Lorna Stevenson

Knowing them

europe books

europe-books.co.uk

ISBN 979-12-201-0198-1
First edition: November 2020

Knowing them

CHAPTER 1

They were Gods. But of course, we didn't know. We didn't see the superman beneath the glasses. We saw flaws, so we saw humanity.

They were flawed. Perfect and flawed. A seemingly impossible truth, to be both flawed and perfect. A truth only understood by people who have met them, or anyone who has truly been in love. I fit both criteria, because I'm the fucking idiot who loved a God.

Before I found out, I was just normal, normal grades, normal family, overall normal family and pretty normal friends. Though I will admit even my old friends were capable of being bizarre and amazing to behold.

The only reason I did find out was because of a coursework assignment, we were put into random groups, and I was put with *her.* I don't really know why she came to class, my best guess is boredom. It was an English class, that we had the coursework for. It had lectures early in the morning, meaning the uniform was jeans and t shirts, to which most people happily complied, me and my friends included. Not her, that classmate, she showed up in dresses and skirts. Not short ones, that would be obvious, and not tight ones. The skirts always flowed around her, skimming her knees in the way that makes you look even if you're the type of guy that doesn't look, in the way that makes you feel like you shouldn't look. Her hair was always up, in a beautiful mess, always with one rose gold wave escaping down her neck, again making you look.

So, anyway, we got put together for an assignment, well us and three others, but one was an airhead of the socialite bitch variety, and the other 2 were of the never going to class variety. So really it was just us, meaning she walked right up to me after class and stood next to my group of friends patiently waiting, she was probably only patient because they were not going to make her wait long. I'm not a nerd in the classic sense, I'm not bookish and I don't play video games, but my friends and I have still got that air about us, which could be because of our general reaction to close encounters with girls. They practically bowed passed her, giving her room to talk to me. With one of my friends looking back at me, mouthing, "Good luck, Will," while giving me a thumbs up, the idiot. She suggested working on it at hers. Suggested while swaying her hips nonchalantly, which made me have to focus a little too much on looking in her eyes, they were a burning gold.

I agreed and now I find myself standing outside a small Victorian house in the middle of a row of identical small Victorian houses. I gulp as I knock on the door, not knowing if I'll be met with strict parents or laid-back roommates and trying to stand with an expression appropriate for both. First appearances cause me way too much stress. But she answers, smiling both adorably and mischievously, she glances down at my shirt and laughs, definitely mischievously.

"Ooh a Doctor Who fan, you're going to love this." She says teasingly, with the laugh still in her voice. I check out my shirt, though I know what I'm wearing, my little sister gave it to me for Christmas, a t-shirt with a TARDIS wearing a fez, I'd always like Matt Smith. I didn't understand her comment, until she opened the door and let me in. Then there was a whole lot more I didn't understand, but her comment wasn't one.

Marble. There was a lot of marble. In the largest reception room, I'd ever seen, it could fit a pool, a big pool, and it wouldn't look out of place. The ceiling was higher than the house had looked to be tall from the outside, and it was two-stories. The floor was a large oval with many doorways leading off into other rooms. A grand staircase started in the middle of the oval and swept gracefully up to a balcony leading to another floor of grandeur. I half expected chandeliers to be hanging from the high ceilings, but there were no visible light fixtures, the room just had light, there weren't even windows for it to come in through. I hadn't stepped over the threshold, I just stayed on the edge. The line that suddenly seemed to be between reality and dream, reason and insanity. I stood on that line and gaped.

"Go on, make the reference, you know you want to." I'd completely forgotten her for a moment, somehow, but now I focussed on her and the teasing, joyful smile she wore. And of course, I had to say it.

"It's bigger on the inside." It comes out as a croak, because normal speech was not happening right now, normal anything was not happening right now. She laughs again and pulls me over the edge, into the dream, into the insanity. I feel too dark, in my t shirt and dark blue jeans, I feel too dark to exist in that space, in that light.

"Cara!" The shout comes from the staircase. That is her name, Cara.

She looks round, her head turn somehow looking exactly like an eye roll. I look up over her, I'm quite tall, and see a guy standing halfway down the staircase, mid step, cradling an open thick book in his arms. He wears black jeans and a fitted, but not too fitted black vee neck. He is a stark contrast to the white of everything else, on him it looks purposeful, like a compositional choice in a painting. He looks very laid back and relaxed apart from his face, his face is pissed.

He walks down the steps, storming towards us, honestly,

9

I am a little surprised he doesn't teleport down, given how my day was suddenly going. As he approaches, he is almost shouting in her face, "I know you've got those idiotic classes you go to, but why do you keep bringing the humans back here?! You just freak them out and they go all annoying."

"Come on relax, it's just funny, they're faces get so cute." Cara says, smile never wavering.

I suddenly feel that I should be seriously insulted. I was being talked about like a dog. Also had he really just said 'humans' like that? I try to speak but only get as far as "Umm…" before I have to duck. That guy had just thrown the book at me, literally. I dodge it messily and as my heart begins jumping erratically from the horrible excitement, I am also struck with a very jarring feeling in my stomach. As I turn to see where the book had landed, I realise why, there hadn't been any noise from the book hitting the closed door or the floor behind me, also, when had the door closed? The book wasn't anywhere behind me, and in the pristine white room it should've been obvious. I turn back to the pair in front of me, scandalised.

"Yeah, real cute." Says the book thrower, his voice drenched in sarcasm.

I can't lie, I am freaking out, with a million questions on the tip of my tongue, which is feeling too big in my mouth, there are too many questions, not one can reach the forefront of my mind, it's too much to be able to form a thought.

"Danny, lay off him. He'll forget anyway, just let me have my fun." Cara sounds both exasperated and a little pleading speaking to the guy, who must be Danny. But the girl does not do pleading properly, she does it like she's flirting, especially when she says 'fun', if that word had been directed at any of my friends, I think they would've swooned, full on swooned.

Again, I am struck with the feeling I should be offended, I was being talked about like a dog. This time, my attempt at speech comes out as an "Ehh..." but then I notice that the book has appeared back in Danny's hands and my mouth just gives up and drops open.

They continue arguing, but I stop listening. The amount of strangeness going on is overwhelming me, pressing into me in all directions, compressing me. A few minutes ago, somehow only a few minutes ago, I'd been standing outside on a normal street on a normal day, expecting the only abnormal thing to happen, to be spending an afternoon with Cara, who had before all this been a little mysterious. Now I stand in an impossible room, which is impossibly big, with impossible light coming from nowhere. And there is a book that seems capable of disappearing and reappearing. And I'd been referred to, as well as, I guessed, a few other people, as 'the humans'. It was all too weird, and it was being treated far too normally by the people in front of me. As my reality continues to disintegrate around me, I tune back into their conversation.

"I've got to do my homework for this class, Danny. And I have to do group work for it. Why not be more comfortable and do it here? It doesn't make any difference in the end, and if you didn't have to be all knowing and check up on me, it wouldn't bother you." Cara's voice has lost its flirting air and she looks different, still like something you want to look at but for very different reasons.

Her rose gold hair that always had a wavy curl to it, is now redder and wilder. It is still beautiful, but it's more dangerous and fiery than her usual, cute look. The red colour isn't all over, it's spreading slowly through her hair as she gets more agitated, the waves of her hair also become more angled, like electricity is running slowly through the strands. The air in the room feels like it's heating uncomfortably too.

Danny was growing angrier as well, "If you didn't pull stupid stunts like this, I wouldn't feel the need to check up

11

on you. And since you insist on going to those stupid classes with *them,*" The disdain in his voice on that last word comes across loud and clear in the horribly warm room, "You can do the work there, they have libraries and cafes I'm sure you could make yourself comfortable in, rather than going through this pantomime every few days." His voice rumbles out, echoing off the rounded walls of the room, causing a cacophony to surround us. His eyes look thunderous and I think I see sparks jolt through them, a part of the same electricity causing Cara's transformation.

The air in the room is becoming too much to take, it is so thick I feel as though it is the largest elephant in the room in existence, and it will not be ignored. The two of them are just staring at each other now, caught up in an argument that must've been brewing for a long time, and is now completely combusting.

The air has become too much, I bend over and heave, releasing the compression on my stomach that had been tightening like a coiled spring. I heave and retch, but like the book there is no sound of it hitting the floor, it just goes, I don't even see it. Once my stomach seems done with me, I straighten up again, feeling lighter but not light. Really, I just feel numb, caught in this space, nothing feels truly real, not even me. I am so detached from it all, I feel no shame from just throwing up in front of people and there is no confusion left in me to wonder about how the floor remains spotless.

They aren't even looking at me, they're still looking at each other. In this space, I am inconsequential, I have stopped mattering to Cara and Danny's argument, I was the catalyst that started it, I won't be used up in the explosion. The detached feeling stays with me, but the numbness fades as I realise there is nothing stopping me exploring this fiction of a place, except that it might cause me to lose my mind, though that is starting to seem like a moot point.

Before I can get caught up in the stickiness of the condensing air again, I make a dash for the door closest to my right. They don't stop me, they've stopped seeing me. I don't stop running, walking around feels like the wrong approach, this place is like the places only possible in the imagination of a young child, to exist in it, I had to be like one of them, and they would run.

The first room I find myself in is a billiard room, long and rectangular, with three full sized tables placed evenly down it. It's all dark word and low light, with fine stuffed dark leather armchairs and sofas organised around the perimeter. It's straight out of an old-style pub back room in the poshest area of a posh town. I almost stop running but the room ends with another open doorway and it calls out to me louder, than the room itself. I continue for three more rooms, all leading straight off from each other. It isn't a maze or a confusing layout, just a seemingly infinite line. I run through a small cosy tv room with comfy sofas, chairs, bean bags and pillows; a library with ceilings higher than the entry room, winding staircases leading to alcoves, reading nooks and shelves and shelves of books; then a swimming pool, a real-life swimming pool with a jacuzzi by the door I ran in through. I continue running, though the urge to do a cannonball on my way back flashes across my mind.

I reach the fourth room and skid to a stop, my heart racing, my mind spinning and my lungs screaming. I stop because I have to, this is not a room to run through, sprint past, and anyway, I'm not the only one in here.

It's a dance studio, with polished wood floors and a bar along one wall, it is definitely a dance studio but strangely there are no mirrors, I hadn't seen any mirrors anywhere so far. A girl stands in the middle of the room, a new face, but she is turned away from me and makes no reaction to me clattering into the room. She is perfectly still, a white figure in a thin pale, pale blue summer dress, with white blonde straight hair falling halfway down her back in a sheet. She looks like a ghost in flesh, no, like a faded memory made solid, just one step from translucence.

As I study her, she starts dancing. There is no music, but she doesn't need it, it comes through anyway. Her arm stretches slowly and gracefully from her side, up and out into the air around her, and as it moves, I *feel* the tug of violin strings, a long soulful wail. Then her whole body turns in a circle, one leg kicking out from the fluttering skirt and making an arch as she spins, the violin picks up into a less pained wail. And as she continues to move, other instruments join the violin. Her feet cross the floor on pointe, each little step a pluck on the keys of a piano, her torso and hips sway and there are light beats of a drum that I feel in my chest. With each move of her delicate fingers, there is the twinkling of a triangle. Her body is an orchestra. I don't hear any of it, that's not it, I feel it, I feel my body react to it. My chest, my heart, my bones, muscles and whole being, everything pulled by that music. Like it's reaching into me, that sweet melody that contains all the horror and beauty of life.

As she stops, so does the music, and I shatter. Tears begin to fall silently down my cheeks. I don't cry often, I save my tears for when they are necessary, but today, today has been…The tears fall faster.

She comes over to me, like a fog crossing over water, her feet make no noise as they approach. Her face is beautiful, slim but curved at all the edges, her nose and mouth petite and rounded too. Her eyes are large, and they are pale too, just like the rest of her, ice blue without the piercing quality that colour tends to have. Even her pupils are pale, the black of them seemingly fogged over. She is blind, I think, just as she reaches me and lifts her hands to my cheeks and lightly brushes the tears from them, with only a whisper of a touch to my own skin. No, she sees more than I do.

The pulling in my body has stopped, now I feel put together wrong. Her face is full of empathy, like she understands, sees through the scramble of my mind, though she can't know anything. But she can answer one thing, the one question that has beaten out the million others to overtake my brain. The question that I felt it would not help to have the answer to, but I was losing my mind, I could almost feel it slipping away, I just needed one concrete truth. So, I ask, my voice shaking and quiet, "What are you people?"

CHAPTER 2

Her response slaps me across the face. I stumble back, her hand reaches out and takes hold of my arm, gently, very gently. She is murmuring that it's okay, repeating the words so they might wash over me and ease the shock, but her previous words are washing over me, making me reel, "You call us Gods."

It couldn't be true, it just couldn't. And not because I was an atheist and didn't believe, because this wasn't what the Gods would be if you met them. It wouldn't be a tease, a jerk and an angel, they were normal.

Except they weren't, not really. Their faces were perfectly unblemished, not just that they were pretty, they were like Disney animations, everything smooth and welcoming. The way they moved, well the way she moved, no human moved like that, I'd seen ballet and I'd liked it well enough, but I hadn't been torn apart by it, even the way Cara moved, it had more impact than simply a pretty girl would. And the book, that disappearing act it had pulled, that could have been Danny. And this place! This place was so grand and implausible, it was fit for the freaking Gods.

I begin sinking into the floor behind me, not literally, though I wouldn't put it passed this place. I am just falling, my knees giving in on me. I can't take this, then a memory comes back to me, of Cara yelling at Danny, a possible saviour from all this.

"Wait, she...she said I would forget all this, I can forget you right?" My voice comes out trembling and scared.

Her face becomes a little sad, but her forehead doesn't crease, and her mouth doesn't quite frown, she seems incapable of making her face look that sad, it just appears around those pale eyes of hers. "Yes, you'll forget when you leave. Mostly, it'll stick around in you like a fading dream" The last word strikes me, and I straighten up, towering over her body which had bent to my level. There's another, even better, more likely solution to all this.

"This is just a dream isn't it?" My voice is now strong and accusing, having an idea I can understand giving me strength, "I'm just having a weird as hell dream, I'm not actually losing it." That had to be it, anything could happen in dreams, I'd just picked up from something normal like class and then gone on a trip, I was going into that stage of waking up were I became a bit aware of the dream and I'd wake up soon.

"Yes, that's it. You're dreaming, just walk outside and you'll wake up." She straightens up too, her head tilting a little to one side as she speaks to me. That knocked the wind out of me again, everything this girl said spun my head in different directions. Because that's not how dreams worked, walking through a door didn't wake you up, you just woke up, and I feel very real, even thinking I'm dreaming I still feel real in my body standing as I am, but I have to be dreaming, nothing else makes sense.

I decide it doesn't matter; I need out. Turning away from that girl, whose name I haven't even asked, I run back the way I'd come, through the pool, not stopping to cannonball like I'd promised myself, through the library, the tv room, the billiard room and finally back into the entrance. Cara and Danny have vanished, to finish their fight elsewhere or to look for me, I'm not sure. I ignore it, and head straight for the door, yanking it open and practically falling out onto the street.

And, I don't wake up, I don't forget. I turn back to the Victorian house, which still looks like the rest of the houses on the street and want to scream. What is happening? Seriously? Reality slams back to me, now I'm out, making the things I've just seen seem even more impossible and wrong. I don't move for a long time, standing facing that façade, weighing what I can do. There aren't many options; go back inside which is nuts, go to the police which is even more nuts since I doubt they'd believe me or be happy with me taking up their time, or go for the old classic and ignore it.

I want an easy life. I start walking down the street, back the way I'd come, shaking my head as I go, trying to come to terms with my newfound insanity. People give me very funny looks as I pass them, which I don't understand until I catch my reflection in a shop window. I look wrecked, my t shirt is drenched in sweat, my face is flushed and gaunt looking, with my eyes sticking out a bit too much. I look sick, but then remember I threw up not that long ago and realise fully that for what I've been through in the last half an hour or so, I look pretty damn good. The looks bother me though, so I pick up my walking to a quick jog as I head home. I pass a bus stop and I feel the sudden need to really go home, so I wait round a bit, fidgety as I do, which doesn't help with the looks I'm getting, and get on a bus out of town, heading towards my parent's place.

Their house looks the same as always as I walk towards it an hour and a half later. I have the keys with me, like always, because I'm never away long enough to bother taking them off my everyday set. There are no shouts of 'Hello' when I enter so I figure everyone must be out. I leave the keys by the door, as a sign I'm in, and head straight upstairs to the shower. I stay in there for a long time, hearing my family come home after only a few minutes, I try to scrub off the day I've had and just let the water run over me once my skin is pink and raw. When I eventually get out, I feel a little better, I towel my hair dry while staring at myself in the mirror. It's stuck up in light brown spikes like it always does when it's wet, and the rest of my face has returned to its normal state, I look like me again, except that my green eyes look a little older to me than they normally do.

After getting dressed, I head right for my little sister's room, Katie is sitting on her bed brushing the hair of a doll, my mum refuses to buy barbies. My heart melts into a puddle at the bottom of my chest when she notices me in the doorway and jumps up excitedly. She moves over to hug me, "Will!" She catches me in a tackle hug around the knees and I chuckle as I bend basically doubled over to hug her back.

I wrestle her off my legs and swoop her up into the air, "Hey Kit Kat, let's take a break." It's a lame joke, but she always explodes like it's hilarious, making it my favourite joke ever. Her laughing descends into coughing, so I carefully move her down into my arms before settling myself onto the bed with her on my lap, rubbing her back as I do.

Expectedly, a shout comes from my mum downstairs, "William, don't over excite her. Please!" She sounds more exasperated than usual, so I shout down an apology rather than my usual grunt.

Katie's breathing is back to normal, but she looks a lot more tired than she had before the hug, and after looking at the clock over my shoulder I realise it's a lot later than I thought. With the whirlwind today has been, I didn't think it would be that late. Katie is looking up at me expectantly, I realise as well that she is in her pyjamas, a smile splits across my face, "So, do you wanna hear a story?" Before she can reply I continue, "Possibly the best story I'll ever tell?" Katie takes an excited intake of breath but I continue again, starting to use my announcer voice, "Possibly the greatest story ever told?" I jump off the bed, making her giggle and duck down to her level looking her goofily in the eye, "Full of magic and intrigue, it'll knock your socks off, but are you ready?" Katie has started nodding like a bobble head, big eyes shining. My grin stretches a little wider and I flop back onto the bed next to her. "I guess I'll have to tell you then." She giggles and cuddles up into me, I move my hand and gently take off the scarf wound round her head, I know she finds it uncomfortable when she's lying down, and I have never understood why she wears it anyway. She's Katie, my perfect little sister, she doesn't need to hide anything, not from me, not her bald head or anything else that shows how much of a warrior she is.

We both settle in, and I tell her the story of my day, I change a lot of it, of course, needing to add in my favourite heroine. I tell her about the palace hidden among the village of a small kingdom, about the fairies who dance in the palace, the demons who scare away visitors and the sirens who bring them there. Katie giggles as I talk about the village idiot who finds himself lost in the palace, running around trying to find a way out, then whoops when I tell her about the brave young knight who rescues him from the maze within. She dozes off as I reach the end of my story and I let my words drift off. I lay there for a while longer, letting myself let the day I've had really become just a story, then I move slowly off the bed and tuck Katie in, she lets out a soft sigh when I leave her, but I move a floppy dog called Winston into my vacated place and she is happy and peaceful again.

I head downstairs and go through to the living room to see my mum, she's sitting on the sofa staring blankly at a soap I know she isn't really watching. I sit down next to her anyway and attempt to follow the overly dramatic story. We sit like that for a while and then she silently goes through to the kitchen and brings back some snacks, we always do better with food. "We weren't expecting you today." She says, in the mum way of asking why I'm there and if anything's happened without asking an actual question.

"I missed Katie," I say, it's an honest reply, I always miss Katie, it just isn't the whole truth, "Had a bit of a weird day, wanted to be home." I don't know what she'll make of that, but I say it anyway.

She just rubs my shoulder in a motherly way and keeps on eating the biscuits between us. My Dad appears from his study and grumbles about us ruining our appetite before taking a biscuit for himself. In the end, we don't make any dinner but simply gorge ourselves on snack food until my dad accepts defeat and heads for bed. My mum follows shortly after him, but I stay down for a while, letting my brain go numb with another mindless tv show that has come on. I can't be bothered heading back to my flat this late, so I set an alarm on my phone to wake me up early enough to compensate for the extra journey time, and settle in for a night on the sofa, not having enough energy to reach my room upstairs.

CHAPTER 3

My alarm doesn't wake me up, but Katie bouncing on my stomach does instead. I have an early class, so have to run around grabbing my shoes and jacket, realising as I look around frantically that I don't have my bag and I can't remember having it passed when I walked into that house yesterday. I must have left it there. Cursing myself, internally, so Katie won't pick up any bad language, I shout a quick goodbye to everyone and make a run for the bus, the stupid things are only hourly.

I make the bus, just, I have to pound the door once to get the driver to open it, and I collapse into a seat, my left leg jiggling up and down for the whole journey as I debate what to do about my bag, both hoping that Cara will bring it to class and that she'll ignore me. I can buy new books. Our English class has at least a hundred and fifty people in it, ignoring people is easy to do.

However, I'm not that lucky, I arrive at the lecture a little early and there Cara is, stood just inside the door, lazily bouncing my bag off her knee, wearing her normal get up of a skirt and a button up shirt, sleeves rolled to the elbow. She grins teasingly as I approach her and holds out the bag to me, "You left this at mine, must've been eager to leave." I take the bag a little roughly, not wanting to interact with her too long.

"Yeah I wonder why." I reply in an undertone, moving quickly passed her and unable to look her in the eye. My face has to show how freaked out I am by being close to her, it's like being back in that room, with all of reality all twisted up, and her and that guy Danny, yelling at each other like I was some stray brought in for amusement.

I hear her mutter something behind me, but I have honestly no interest in what it is. I head to my seat, my friends, Ian and Jack, sitting there looking confused by me not taking on the flirting opportunity with Cara. I decide to play it cool and just shrug at them. Throughout the class I feel both their eyes on me and Cara's, but I just sit and listen to our lecturer, Martin Crawford, harder than I ever have. He is a pretty decent lecturer, but he gets a bit too excited about the subject, going off on so many tangents it's difficult to keep track of what he's actually on about. He starts working through an analogy, that I am sure would've related to the lecture somehow in about 5 minutes, if he hadn't stopped talking.

And moving, and breathing, just like everyone else in the lecture theatre stops doing, all at once.

I whip my head around, able to hear the noise it makes in the very uncomfortable quiet. Cara has stood up, and is walking towards me, walking over the tops of the desks of the suddenly statuesque students. I'm frozen too, but not like they are, I am frozen by the dread that this is real. Because that means that yesterday hadn't been a story and they are, she is, what that girl had called them, said we called them, they were Gods.

"You aren't meant to remember." Cara says, her voice imperious and rich, with an almost perfectly hidden trace of worry.

"I didn't want to." I reply, my own voice seeming like nothing compared to her, though I guess I am.

She's reached me by now and stands on the desk in front of me, crouching down so her face is just a little above mine. Her pose reminds me bizarrely, of a gargoyle crouched on top of a building, of a guardian spirit, and I've messed with

23

her duties "We can fix that." She whispers to me, reaching her hand out to cup my cheek. I unfreeze at that instant and stand up, needing her not touch me.

"No." Her face mirrors my own shock as I say it, I hadn't meant to say it, but I did mean it. "I can't just forget. I mean, I want to, but I feel like you owe me more."

Cara shoots up too, "Owe you?!" She barks back at me, her hair becomes a little red like it had before.

"Yes, owe me. You're Gods, she said you were Gods. I need to know what that means. I want to understand. Please. Okay I'd like to know." I've turned pleading now, I think of myself as an atheist, which has been ruined by recent events, but that doesn't mean I'm ready to get down on my knees and bow to the Gods. But I do need to understand what this is. For Katie. If they are who they seem to be, they let that happen. They let her hurt, were letting her hurt, in a way I'd do anything to stop. I have to know if I should be angry at them or continue just being angry.

Maybe, it shows on my face, the desperation that goes beyond morbid curiosity, because she deflates slightly, and her hair turns back to its less angry hue.

"There are going to be a lot of conditions attached." There is a faint smile on Cara's face as she says it, and despite the adrenaline running around my veins, after making demands of a possible all-powerful being, and her sudden U-turn, I let out a little laugh in response before I nod.

Cara's eye bore deep into my soul as she continues, "No discussing what you learn with anyone, ever." The last word is laced with threat. "You can't remember everything forever, there'll be an impression left but we can't let you remember details." She leaves a little pause for me to argue at this point, or possibly to voice confusion but I'm just holding my breath for her to let me know anything, "Okay, after classes you may come to our home and host a few interviews. Just a few."

Cara seems finished, so I think over the whole deal. Not talking about them seems fair, for worry of being put in an asylum, I wasn't planning on saying anything anyway. Having an impression of what I find out might be enough, remembering everything would probably be too much anyway, I'm already having enough trouble dealing with all this. The only thing that seems odd is having the basically open invitation to show up at their home, and not having any limits placed on what I can ask. But it's what she said, and I feel like I've pushed my luck enough. I nod again.

The class snaps back into place, Crawford keeps talking, and I feel my friend, Ian, next to me, pulling on my sleeve to get me to sit down again. As I do, I turn to slyly look at Cara, she is back in her seat from earlier and looks like she's paying attention to the lecture, but as I look away, just out the corner of my eye, I see her wink.

The rest of the day is a whirlwind for me, I'm only half in it, drifting in and out, thinking about what the evening could turn into. Ian is a good distraction, we've known each other since primary school, so there's an unspoken agreement of no judgement, meaning he ignores it when I act a bit like a zombie for a day.

Instead, he spends the time we all eat lunch getting us caught up on his plans for his 19th, Ian has always been the youngest in our group of friends, so goes all out for his birthdays, his 18th went down in history as the only party any us had been to that necessitated both the fire service and police being called. Everything was okay in the end, but Ian became a legend. He's been talking through his expansive guest list, which I was mostly ignoring until he mentions Cara. I snap my head towards him in surprise, hoping he is kidding, but sadly no.

"Come on Will, a party with her would be a riot. And

you've got that study time with her, couldn't you ask?" Ian is practically doing a puppy dog face as he says it.

I sigh and think a bit before I answer his pouting face, "I'm studying with her tonight, but-"

He cuts me off. "Perfect! You can ask tonight. The worst she can say is no." I sigh again, wishing I'd thought longer before speaking, but Ian gets up and moves quickly away from our table, heading to his next class very early, obviously to avoid my rebuttal. I will ask her, I can't not, but Ian owes me.

The evening ahead already has all the signs of being incredibly weird and awkward, without a party invitation attached.

My last class of the day is Philosophy, it's just a typical first year introduction to philosophy, having us read Descartes, the 'I think therefore I am' guy and contemplate what it is to think. I'd taken it because all the other elective options sounded worse, but today it feels like my most important class.

I watch the lecturer striding back and forth and just copy the notes on the board, not any of his little additions and explanations that I am normally frantic to get down for help. My mind is too full of yesterday, and his words are making me wonder if philosophy might help me avoid being sectioned.

CHAPTER 4

After the class ends, as I walk slowly back to that street from the day before, my mind is still adjusting to what I'd seen there, thinking about how they could be really possible and everything else that might be possible.

My heart is speeding up in panic when my phone buzzes unexpectedly in my pocket. Which doesn't help. I jump like a timid cat that's just been petted, as buzzing takes over the music I've been listening to and I stop walking to check it.

I'm always too nervous to use my phone while walking, I'd been doing it once a few years ago and almost fell over a little yappy dog because I hadn't seen him under my feet. I got an earful from his owner, an old woman with a voice so shrill I swear it's still rattling my ears.

It's a text from Ian, "Remembering to ask right??" I smile down at my phone, shaking my head a little at his excitement at the possibility of Cara joining us for a party. Though I guess, two days ago I would've been right on his side about it being a great idea. I text back that I am indeed remembering, then start walking again, pressing the button on the side of my phone to increase the volume of my music. Ian's text knocked me out of the spiral of thoughts I'd been stuck in, and I want to keep it that way, music too loud to think feels like the way to go.

Cara is sitting outside the house when I arrive. She's perched on the low wall that separates the house from the street, her hands resting against the back of it, leaning back in a pose almost like sunbathing. She's changed out of her clothes from earlier and is for the first time, casual, sporting blue skinny jeans, with red converse and a sleeveless, floaty long shirt. I am so surprised by the non-flirty way she is dressed that I don't pause my music as I reach her, I simply stop hearing it.

She grins at the sight of me, and hops up, taking my earphones off my head so she can say hello. I grin sheepishly back at her, put at ease from my caution of the whole walk over. "Are you ready?" Cara asks, her voice similar to the announcer tone I use when playing with Katie, my grin grows slightly but I don't laugh like she would have.

"Honestly, I don't think I could be." I reply jokily. It's a bit like when I'd been in the house before, in their presence, in this place, everything doesn't seem as strange. It is still definitely a strange situation, but one that feels oddly like a dream, one so apart from reality it must be without danger, without consequence. Everything about Cara right then, her warm smile, her tone, her appearance, are all calming me down, with only a small part of my brain worried that that might stem from what she is. I don't know what she is capable of, yet.

Her hand takes mine and I feel a tingle of electricity, one that makes me feel connected to her, through more than mere touch. She'd laughed lightly at my answer and seems to feel, quite rightly, the necessity to walk me through the door.

The room is almost the same, except for a grand piano now resting in the middle of it, in front of the base of the stairs, which is so bizarre it works perfectly in the room.

"Can you play?" Cara asks, following my gaze and releasing my hand, stopping the current passing between us.

"Can't you tell?" I ask in return, taking it upon myself not to wimp out of finding out a little about what they are. I haven't totally forgotten my purpose in being here, despite the light tone I sincerely use.

"Good first question. And no, I can't." Cara laughs again as she informs me, she strides over to the piano and jumps seamlessly up to sit on it, crossing her legs as she does so and clasping hands at her knees. She looks me dead on, swishing her loose rose gold hair over her shoulder. "Next."

I stand there and think. Trying despite the feeling of calm in my head, to sort through everything I want to know. What does it mean that they are Gods? What can they do? Where did they come from? When did they come from? How many of them are there? What kind of Gods are they? What are they responsible for? What do they feel responsible for? On and on my mind spins with questions, which all feel like they demand answering. But I don't know how many I'll have the chance to ask and there is always the possibility she won't be honest.

As I continue to just stand there, with my head spinning out beyond me, Cara sits patiently waiting, but that lasts less than 30 seconds. Before I manage to get anything out, she hops down from the piano, seeming decisive and possibly a little irritated. Cara never struck me as being sincerely patient.

"Why don't I give you a starting point?" She asks, walking away from me before I can answer, heading around the staircase, behind it to a doorway directly opposite the entrance. I hurry to catch up with her, moving clumsily around the piano, which I can't play in case you're wondering.

The room we walk into isn't a room at all. It appears to be outside, though I doubt it truly is. It looks like a garden, a true garden of Eden, large and wild looking yet aesthetically perfect. Nothing is too much; the trees are scattered in a way allowing for both a feeling of openness and seclusion. Flowers of every colour are everywhere, but not in a way that limits the space to walk around without risking trampling them and their beauty. The sun above us is bright and warm, not hot or so strong that shade is required.

Cara is unfazed by the beauty of it all and doesn't miss a beat in continuing to walk on. I stumble a little, tripping over my feet, caught between the desire to bask in this place and to see where I am being led, what starting point I'm being given.

It turns out I'm being taken to an open, simply grassy area of the garden where the dancer from the day before and a guy different from Danny sit on a picnic blanket. This new guy has dark skin, very short black hair and a thick set build. His face looks perfectly passive and perfectly nice. Except for his left cheek, which has a long narrow scar along the cheek bone, it looks old and not like it would be painful but staring at it makes me feel an odd stab of guilt deep in my stomach.

I am distracted from my staring at his cheek by the dancer moving over to me and cupping my right cheek. Her touch is light, as is her voice. "It's good to see you again Will." She almost whispers, "I'm sorry we scared you yesterday and that I lied to you." She is so honest in her apology that I want to rush to tell it isn't necessary, but I also know there is no need. She is made of empathy, she knows.

Being with her and Cara at the same time is strange to me, Cara is so bold and defined next to the other, so much wilder as well. And the guy next to her is so dark in comparison, but the contrast between them seems to balance like Yin and Yang. And though she stands with her face turned to me, and he stands apart from her not really looking at anything, I can feel the bond between them, like it is a part of the air.

I felt at peace here, looking between them, my eyes settle on the girl and I decide to start at the beginning. "What's your name?"

A little smile blossoms on her face, "I'm Lily." It suits her, no other name would have worked for a face that sweet. My parents planned on calling Katie Lily, but when she arrived, she was so loud, they agreed that a peaceful name wouldn't suit her, I had to agree.

"Nice to meet you Lily," I say, smiling at her and nodding my head once, I turn to look at the guy behind her and outstretch my hand to him. "I'm Will." I've never been so formal in my life, but it fits here.

He grips my hand and shakes it, but he doesn't speak. Lily speaks for him instead. "This is Sam." She says, it suits him too, a good dependable name.

We release each other's hands and I look between the three of them. The peaceful feeling stays with me, but a laugh bubbles up in my throat. It's all so ridiculous. Lily focuses her eyes on me, full of understanding as they always seem to be. I swallow my laughing and ask the biggest question of the moment. "How?" I glance around at all of them again and the garden we are in, as I stretch out the single syllable, I try to encapsulate everything I mean.

They all laugh a little, and the girls, should I call them girls, fall in unison to sit on the grass. Sam following a step behind them, me a step behind him.

"How? Where to start?" Says Cara, glancing around the place as I did. "For one, this place, it's not real, well it's not reality." She pauses again, looking at my face which has crumpled in confusion, "I mean, it exists, you are for all intents and purposes in this garden, all your senses feel like you're here." Her voice is a mixture of matter-of-fact and soothing, but I don't feel soothed. My head is already hurting the way it does in my philosophy class when the difference between mind and brain is explained.

I try though, "So, my mind is here, so I am, but physically I'm not here?" My voice comes out slowly, carefully, it feels like a philosophy lesson all of a sudden, but I guess that is part of what we are discussing.

Lily nods encouragingly, "In essence, yes." I nod back at

her, deciding to go with it. Unsure if I want to know where I really am.

"But how?" I ask, it dawning on me, that I might get stuck in a spiral of hows if I'm not careful.

Lily smiles and takes that question for herself. "We make this place, honestly we can't explain a how to you for this, but we feel it and here it all is. Like genie wishes." She adds in at the end, trying to help me out.

I think for a moment about that. I couldn't really argue with them, but it was a lot to just take. "So, you're magic?" I ask, running with the genie example.

Cara shakes her head, hair bouncing in annoyance, while Lily nods at her side. Sam doesn't do anything. The girls look at each other, "We're not freaking witches." Cara says, her voice holding the subtle undertone of a hiss.

"And we can explain that, but it's close enough." Lily rallies, her voice even as ever. These girls really are opposites of each other. They continue to stare at each other for a few moments, then turn back to me, as though a decision has been reached, but I'm not sure what the decision is. I don't ask, and instead silently choose to go with Lily and take it as magic.

Wanting to change the direction of the questioning, I ask, "How many of you are there?" All of them cast their eyes down for a second and I glimpse Cara's eyes momentarily flit to red, rather than gold as she looks back up. "There are six of us, it used to be seven. That was a long time ago." Her last words hold so much sadness, I let that road end there.

"There's two more I haven't met?" I ask instead.

Lily smiles approvingly and answers that time, it's like her and Cara had agreed to take turns, while Sam is a silent overseer. "Yes, there's a chance you'll meet them both today. Ivy's very excited to meet you." The tone she uses when mentioning Ivy makes me picture her as an excitable young child, but I assume she won't be, being one of them.

"I'm sure I'm excited to meet her too." As I say it, I realise it's the first thing I've said in a while which isn't a question and I began to feel a little guilty. These people are being perfectly nice to me and I'm not properly talking *to* them.

Lily notices my change in mood. "Why don't we go find her?" It might've sounded patronizing, but Lily doesn't seem capable of anything that negative.

I nod, and we all stand up, me moving on the same beat as Sam this time. The girls walk ahead, and I fall in step with him. I ask yet another question but try to keep it friendly, "Do you ever talk?"

Sam grins and shakes his head. I don't mind, his silence is warm rather than cold. It feels like the reason he matches with Lily. The way they both are, they could've been scary; his strong presence dominated by silence, her ghostly pale figure that seems to inhabit within your mind when looking at you, but somehow, they are just kind.

I can't make up my mind about Cara, she has warmth, yes, but it only seems to reach up to a point and then turns into wild fire, easily capable of getting someone hurt and not easy to tame.

We walk back through to the entrance area. Where the piano no longer sits, "Where's the piano?" I ask, it is so hard not to ask questions in a place like this.

"Piano?" Lily asks, turning her head back towards me, I'm a little stunned there is something she doesn't know.

"Danny was playing earlier, hadn't bothered to get rid of it before Will arrived." Cara offers, like it is nothing for a Grand piano to bounce around a house.

I smirk a little and manage to catch Sam's eye, he is smirking back at me.

We all stop walking when we reach the centre of the room,

and Cara spins in a slow circle, apparently deciding how to call for Ivy. She goes for the classic.

"IVY!" She shouts, screwing up her pretty face against the noise, before it relaxes back into smooth perfection. "That should get her right?" She asks too innocently. We all laugh.

CHAPTER 5

For all I know, this place continues infinitely, which could mean sound wouldn't carry that far into it. Then again, if they're capable of making infinity, they can probably make sound reach through it.

As we wait, Cara strides back in between Sam and me, and flops casually onto a comfy leather sofa behind us which hadn't been there before. I almost roll my eyes; it's quickly becoming less shocking to observe the disappearing/appearing acts around here. I instead move over and sit down on the other end of the seat. I have to fight a sigh, it's so comfortable. It eases the knot in my back I didn't know I had.

Lily and Sam follow suit, sitting together on an identical sofa which appears 90 degrees round from ours, by my side. They take up only half of the seat, as Lily nestles into Sam's side. I'd suspected they were together, but it's sweet to see a confirmation. They fit together.

We sit in comfortable silence for a few moments, me enjoying the memory-foam like comfort of the leather. Despite the fact we're waiting, it still seems very sudden when she appears. A rainbow blur buzzes into the room and zips over to hug me. I had melted deep into my seat, but she manages to wrap her arms around my neck. I try to hug her back, well, to pat her back awkwardly, which is the best affection I can show strangers, but she moves too quickly.

She stands up straight and although she stops moving, it somehow looks like she's still bouncing. I am lost for words as I take in her appearance.

Purple hair, light but not lilac, possibly violet, cut into a spiky pixie cut. Caramel skin that looks artfully roughened from being constantly outdoors. Jade green eyes, that sparkle like actual gemstones caught in the perfect light. A green, red and yellow thick striped jumper, baggy at her neck and wrists but tight where it ends, just above her midriff. Bell bottom jeans, with square patches sewn on, of swirled patterns of green and purple. Completed with a pair of orange doc marten boots. All of this in a 5ft2 smiling figure.

She is the picture of a perfect hippy. Looking both straight out of the sixties, as well as from the group that organises all the rallies at my university.

"Ivy?" I say to her, not really a question since she looks exactly like an Ivy. Her head bobs up and down, and she starts to properly bounce.

"And you're Will." She bursts out, bending down to hug me again, I'm more prepared this time and manage to pat her left shoulder once before she releases me. "How're you enjoying getting to know us?" Ivy asks, placing herself on the arm of Lily and Sam's sofa. Her legs either side of it, hands on the edge, fingers tapping fidelity.

"Um, it's been interesting." I say, smiling, not sure myself what kind of interesting I mean. But thinking about it for a moment, I realise it is a good one. I've been smiling and laughing with all these people since I got here. Maybe I hadn't gone into the interrogation of them that I'd been expecting and dreading, but I can't deny I'm having fun.

My smile grows as I think about it, and everyone else is smiling too.

"We are definitely interesting." Muses Cara, enjoying the word.

"Personally, I find the humans way more interesting." Says Ivy, leaning back a little.

"Yeah, because that's where you get all your fads." Cara

retorts, her smile turning to a smirk. "You're such an eternal hipster."

I turn back to Ivy, who is suddenly wearing thick black rimmed hipster glasses. She takes hold of them at one side and pulls them down the bridge of her nose. "You know it." She says, waggling her eyebrows as she does, and then tossing the rims at Cara playfully. Who fumbles in a very girly manner trying to catch them.

We all bust up laughing, it feels like when I go for lunch after class, sitting in a group together, laughing at utter nonsense.

Cara tries to throw the glasses back at Ivy but misses horribly and hits Sam in the chest. Our laughing hitches up a gear.

Just as we are beginning to settle down again, my phone buzzes in my pocket, making me jump comically in response, and causing the others to explode again. "I didn't expect a signal in here." I say through my dying laughter as I fish my phone out of my pocket.

"We wish for it, so it shall be." Says Lily, opening up her arms like in offering.

Cara snorts, somehow not unattractively. "Stop with the genie stiff."

Looking down at my phone, successfully free from my pocket, I see a text from Ian. "You check with her yet?" It takes me a moment of staring at the screen to figure out what he means. The party, he wants to know if I've asked Cara about coming yet. I had totally forgotten. I smirk at the fact he hadn't waited long to check but then realise I've been there for over an hour; it's felt like ten minutes.

I look back up and round at them all. "Sorry, I've got to go. I hadn't realised the time," My words are met with a few blank looks, for a second the concept of time mattering is lost on them. "Could we do this again? Tomorrow or something?" I ask, nervous they'll say no.

"Of course." Says Lily, as Cara stands to show me out.

"We've got the time to spare." Adds Ivy, an odd mix of sadness and humour in her voice. I look over at her as I stand, trying to read her expression, but her smile is genuine and her eyes clear and open.

So, I look away from her and begin following Cara to the door, lifting my hand in a lazy wave as I pass the others, which Sam returns.

My feet are either side of the threshold when I remember I still haven't asked about the party, "Cara," I begin, my mouth suddenly dry, "There's this party my friend, Ian, is throwing for his birthday, he wanted you to come." As I finish speaking, I realise I hadn't phrased it as a question. Figures, I've asked questions the whole time I'm here but fail now. Social awkwardness rears its head for me with parties.

Cara tilts her head, considering my statement, and possibly trying to place who on Earth Ian is. A small smile lights her face. "We'd love to come." The use of 'we' surprises me, but the door is being closed on me.

I guess it will be fine if they all come, Ian will allow anything for Cara to go. So, I accept it and turn to leave, as I do, I catch the sight of something out the corner of my eye. I turn back with just enough time to see what it is before the door eclipses my view and clicks shut, pushing me into the real world.

It'd been on the landing, far above the entrance floor, leaning against the balcony. A girl, another girl. The sight of whom meant only one word fills my mind as I stand on the steps outside.

Woah.

CHAPTER 6

I call Ian on my way back from the house to tell him, not about the 'woah' that is echoing around my mind bouncing through every crevice of it, just about Cara. He whoops, quite literally whoops down the line to me, I pray he isn't in public.

The two days after that are spent sorting out the party and buying a frightening amount of booze to stock Ian's parents' house. I haven't been able to go back to Cara's house again, my evenings are all about the prep, I even have to help Ian pick out his outfit for the night. Not my area of expertise, I just go for a clean pair of jeans, a red t shirt and a denim jacket myself. That's what I'm wearing as I stand again in front of that old Victorian house for the third time.

It's Saturday night, really evening as night hasn't fallen yet. I'm here to pick them up for the party, Cara joked with me in class the day before about needing an escort and I decided not to take it as a total joke.

I knock hesitantly on the door, not knowing how loud a knock I need for them to hear me.

A new face opens the door. I groan inwardly that there is another one, but once I look into the jade green eyes staring at me, I rethink my groan.

"Ivy?" I ask. Everything else is different on the person standing in front me, who has long lilac hair, a paler shade of tan skin and is a little taller, but the eyes are too similar, identical.

The new face grins. "Good eye Will." Her voice is exactly

the same as before. I look her up and down a few times before she offers my gaping face an explanation. "It's a big night out, I thought I'd mix things up for it. Forgot that bit was new to you" Ivy seems very amused by my reaction.

My eyes are wide open, and my mouth is the same, it's difficult to just accept that they can change faces! But I take a steadying breath and focus on the green eyes, remembering what my mum always tells Katie and I about looks, that they don't matter except for the eyes, as long as your eyes are kind, you are beautiful. It's cheesy as anything, but it helped Katie when she started losing her hair, and it helps me now. Those green eyes are definitely kind, so I stop making a weird face and step with her into the house.

"Do you do that often?" I ask. "Mix things up." I try to have my voice be casual, but it comes out a little hoarse anyway.

Ivy laughs to herself before speaking, "Yeah, quite a bit. Way more than the others. Been around a long time and I'm still trying to find myself." She looks at the floor when she says it, almost like she's embarrassed. I bump my arm against hers.

"Pretty sure everyone in the world is on the same boat with you there." I say, grinning at her. She smiles back at me and the embarrassment abandons her.

The light in the room turns off, and I flinch from the abruptness of it, but a spotlight illuminates the top of the grand staircase a moment later. It showcases Cara standing there, her rosy hair cascading in loose waves down her shoulder, wearing a beautiful dress in dark red, that makes her hair seem to glow in comparison, with a tight bodice and skirt that spreads out a little at her hips extending down to the floor, with a slit in the skirt riding all the way up her right leg.

"What do you think?" Cara asks dramatically, striking a pose. Ivy answers before I have the chance.

"It's a house party not a ball. No." I laugh at Ivy's bluntness, but it's fair answer. Cara snorts, and the lights flash off again.

This time, when the lights click on again, though I still can't see where they are coming from, Cara is now in a bright red dress, ending just above her knees, that hugs her chest and then fans out like the skirts she wears to class. A far simpler dress, in short, to the previous one. She raises her eyebrows for our opinion again, and again Ivy answers before me.

"I guess that's as close as you'll get to casual." She says, dryly. Herself wearing loose bottomed grey jeans, a colourful striped shirt, with long sleeves that hangs off her shoulders, and the orange docs from days before. It's a good casual night out outfit, still a lot more dressed up than I am.

Cara smiles, satisfied, and starts her strut down the stairs. As she does, Danny appears on the landing as well, wearing a designer looking black shirt and black jeans. Does he ever wear anything other than black? That's the first thought that enters my mind, but as he starts down the stairs after Cara, I instead ask, "You're coming too?" My voice deeply incredulous.

Last time he saw me; he'd thrown a book at me. I hadn't expected him to want to party down with me.

"Problem?" He asks in return, not as a question but as a challenge. One I did not want to rise to.

Instead, I roll my eyes, just slightly, too scared of having another book chucked at my head to do it properly and turn to the girls to complement their outfits. They do both look pretty.

However, I don't get the words out. As I open my mouth, a door opens to the left of me and Lily and Sam enter. Lily wearing the same delicate dress I'd seen her wear when I first met her, and Sam wearing a white t shirt and dark jeans. A man after my own fashion sense.

I smile at their entrances, which is returned two-fold. The six of us there stand in a makeshift circle.

"So," Begins Ivy, awkwardly. "Will we just head out then?" She asks, and is met with a chorus of nods from the others.

They all start moving towards the door, but I raise my hands in a simple halting gesture. "Wait, there's one more of you right? I know I haven't met her, but she's welcome to join." I say, keeping close attention to not sound too eager. I'd only glimpsed her the other day and still feel a little high off the buzz of it. I had been hoping she would come too.

"She?" Asks Danny, his face curious and tinged with anger around the crease between his eyebrows. He seems to be wondering how I know the last of them is a girl, I remember they hadn't actually mentioned her gender to me before. And from Danny's face, I apparently am not meant to have had that glimpse of her.

"Ella doesn't really go out." Says Lily, interrupting the staring match that has begun between Danny and me.

I move my head round to Lily, grasping hold of the name, 'Ella', it's a nice name. "Still, but…" I begin but am quickly cut off by Cara.

"Like ever." Her voice is sharp and offers a definitive end to the conversation.

I shut my mouth and decide to leave it, I don't even know this girl and should not risk being late for Ian's party for her. As his essential best friend these days, there is an unspoken rule that I not arrive that late. I go to head for the door but am stopped by the sight of Ivy, who is next to me, ogling the landing above.

Everyone has seen her too, and we all turn in unison to see what has turned Ivy to a comical statue. And there she is.

Standing in the middle of the top step, in a dressing gown, looking as though frozen while being caught on the way to make a late-night cup of tea. Seeing her properly, I almost fall to my knees.

She has long brown hair, almost straight but with just enough wave to it that you can't call it straight, with pale tanned skin that is the perfect shade to show off her eyes. Those eyes. They are a shining azure blue that glows across the distance between us, suddenly seeming to be the source of all the light in the room.

She looks so surprised to see us there, her mouth opens in a small 'o' of shock. My face is matching hers until I somehow am the one to break the silence in the room.

"Hi." I say. The word echoing as a whisper, sweeping the room in waves.

She smiles at me and says hello back. I think I die for a second.

Danny is immediately irritated by our interaction and speaks up. "We're just heading out. We'll be back later, ok?" He says, beginning to move in a way ushering us out the door before he's done talking.

"Come." I say, apparently only capable of one-word sentences when looking at her, at Ella. It's not a question, it's a necessity. I feel like I can't leave the room without her.

Part of my brain is muttering that I don't know anything about her, with another section urging me to get to the party already, for Ian. But the vast majority of my mind is lost in her eyes and has no interest in finding a way out.

Danny ignores my words, well word, and continues his efforts to shove us all to the door. Everyone else begins to move out as well, but they freeze as Ella speaks.

"Ok." She says, her voice full of equal parts resolution and apprehension.

A grin splits across my face, my head screaming yes and fist pumping. And Ella laughs a little at my reaction. She undoes the belt of her dressing gown, taking it off and re-

43

vealing pale blue skinny jeans, with mid-calf brown leather boots and a midnight blue sparkled vest top.

I take a sharp intake of breath and receive a nudge in the ribs from Ivy. I look over to her and she gives me a knowing look, like one of Lily's but with far more amusement in it.

Ella starts down the stairs, and the others who have all been caught in shocked silence since her arrival, begin to talk casually amongst themselves. A little too casually. I try to go with them, and act like it's no big deal, as they obviously think is necessary. I fight to turn my attention away from Ella and to the others.

"Ian's house is a bit far to walk, he lives well outside of town. I was thinking we could get the bus instead." Since I am no longer looking at Ella, it's become a lot easier to speak in full sentences.

Sam lets out a soft, silent chuckle, and Lily gives me a sweet look. "We can drive. Cara doesn't do buses." She glances over at Cara while saying it, who is smiling back, proudly.

We finally make it out the door, me at the front of the group with Ivy, Ella at the back, feeling very far away. "I probably shouldn't be surprised you have a car." I comment to Ivy, who laughs.

"Yeah with us, you should probably raise the bar of surprise, just a bit." I smirk in agreement. My bar has been on a rollercoaster all week.

Ivy leads our group to a pick-up style Jeep. As we get closer to it, my eyes go out of focus as a roof rises up over the back of the truck, seats emerge inside the enclosing bed of it, with doors growing onto the sides and the whole body of the car lowers down to the road. While my eyes refocus, the whole design become more refined. I am now looking at a nice car with plenty of space to carry all of us, one that I am pretty sure doesn't match any known car design.

Sam moves away from Lily, round to the driver's seat, while she and Danny move to take the other two spaces in the front. Cara turns expectantly towards me, and I take my cue to open the door and allow the rest of the girls in. I knew she wasn't totally kidding about the whole escort thing. Cara gracefully slides in and over to the far window, Ivy follows after, more clumsily than Cara and pats my shoulder as she goes. The final two seats face Cara and Ivy's, backing onto the seats in front. Ella eyes them a little suspiciously from my side, I lift my hand to her, to help her in. She takes it and steps cautiously up and in. Her touch is warm, in a way that sooths every nerve I have, a calm washes over me from it. A calm that I wish she had herself.

I move in after Ella, taking the last seat next to her, and shut the door. Ella looks very uncomfortable in her seat, she's buckled her seatbelt but stiffly clings to the edges of the chair either side of her, her petite hands shaking as her knuckles grow white.

"I'm not used to cars." She mutters like an apology to me.

I feel my face melt; the way I'd only felt it do for Katie. Ella reminds me of the worry I'd seen on Katie's face when she was going in for her first MRI. They'd let me stay with her, to talk her into being calm and to not squirm around.

My hand instinctively moves over to Ella's and the last two fingers of my right hand slide over the white knuckles of her left. "It'll be ok." I say, repeating the words I'd spoken over a year ago to my shaking sister, and innumerable times since.

The tension lessens in Ella's shoulders and the corners of her mouth rise, so does a pink in her cheeks.

I move my hand away and turn away, suddenly shy and nervous. I glance over at Ivy and Cara who have been having their own conversation. They both look at me, Ivy smiling knowingly and encouragingly, while Cara smirks knowingly and teasingly. They are like the angel and devil on my shoulders for this situation. Both on my side, but dealing with it very differently. I try to ignore them both and look out the window.

CHAPTER 7

The rest of the journey passes with general car conversation. I'm giving Sam directions when Lily prompts me. Cara and Ivy are trying to explain house party culture to Ella, without much success, they disagree on every point. Danny is relatively silent, just grunting or snorting at various points.

We pull up to the house, probably just a little later than I am meant to arrive, the music and shouting is loud enough to be heard down the street and the first person has already started throwing up in the bushes. Ian's parents decided to have a week away, to both avoid the party and give Ian plenty of time to clear up, so they can pretend they don't know about it. Ian's neighbours have been warned about the upcoming noise, but I doubt they're happy about it. Luckily Ian's dad is a scary man, so they won't say anything, or call the police.

I take the lead again and get out the car first, holding the door for the girls. Ivy gets out and walks right into the house. Cara follows her and goes in with Danny, who has vacated the front seat and offers her his arm. Out the corner of my eye I see Sam and Lily head into the party together, while I duck my head back into the car to check on Ella, who looks completely terrified.

I jerk my head towards the house. "You won't want to miss this," I say, trying to grin encouragingly, "My friend might start actually drooling when he sees Cara here." Ella laughs, and unbuckles her seatbelt.

As we walk up to the entrance, our footsteps automatically become in sync with the beat ricocheting around inside.

Ian's house is frighteningly modern, a stereotypical repercussion of his rich dad and high-strung stay at home mum. Every surface of the house is pristinely white with sharp corners, while all the furniture is in bright block primary colours, made of hard plastic or metal.

I personally hate Ian's house. Whenever I visited it growing up, it just hadn't felt homey to me. Personal items didn't match the décor, so they'd never had any. The house felt cold and unbelievably sad to grow up in to me. It was no surprise that we spent most of our time growing up at mine or our friend Felix's houses.

Ella takes in the house as she stands still, next to me, in the doorway. I see her wrinkle her nose and feel a small rush of glee, at the matched reaction.

It's quickly interrupted, by Ian knocking into my left shoulder and almost sending me flying. I reach out to catch him, and we unsteadily manage to both stay upright. We're the picture of grace and elegance. Ian's eyes take a while to find mine through his haze of drink.

"She came! You actually got Cara to come. Dude, this party is going to rock!" He shouts excitedly to me, over the noise in the room, almost knocking out an eardrum.

I laugh, both because of his excitement and his obvious drunken state. For someone who throws the best parties in town, Ian has never mastered handling his drink. Especially spirits, which, from the stink of the cup in his hand that is thrown round my shoulder, is what he must be drinking.

"I know. On both counts. How much have you had?" I ask, having to shout as well.

He takes his arm from my shoulder and looks into the bowels of his cup, before taking a long swig. "I don't know." He says, when he comes up for air. "But a lot more than you. We must rectify that." He doesn't manage to pronounce 'rectify' properly.

Ian starts leading me through the crowd of people in the room, which isn't easy, as they are so tightly packed, they practically form a solid. The whole ground floor of the house is open plan, combining entrance with a living area to the right, dining room to the left and extensive kitchen area taking up the back half of the space. With a wide staircase leading upstairs, running along the right wall.

As Ian pulls me to the kitchen for a drink, I turn back to get Ella to join us, but she's vanished.

I wonder for a moment about going to search for her, but I don't feel that I can leave Ian, and figure that one of the others has probably found her. So, I allow myself to be dragged.

We reach a large cooler which has been placed on the kitchen island. I fish my hand in and withdraw a cider. I like to start slow with my drinking. Which I get a lot of crap for, but I also spend less time hungover than my friends, so that's ok by me.

"How's the birthday going?" I ask, as I take a bottle opener from the counter by my side and prise off the cap.

"Aw it's great. I'll remember nothing." Says a grinning Ian, in drunken bliss. Just then, a girl, Jackie, from our lunch table, rushes passed us in a whirl of black curls and throws up in the sink, turns on the tap for a sip of water, then straightens up and heads right back into the crowd.

"Probably for the best." I say, patting Ian's shoulder.

We spot another friend of ours dancing in the middle of the crowd. Ian and I head over and begin dancing with him. Now, normally I'm not big on dancing, but since everyone here is plastered and won't remember, plus I can't possibly look as bad as Ian, I let myself go for it.

I soon feel the faint effect of the cider and the atmosphere hit me, and I loosen up my dancing a bit more. As I do, I feel a tap on my shoulder and I turn around to see Ivy.

"Mind if I join?" She asks, happily, raising her voice over the music.

I smile and move wordlessly around to include her in the small circle of dancing we've got going on. She starts mimicking me and my friend's dorky moves, laughing as she does. We all laugh with her and I see Ian and our friend, Jack, introduce themselves to her. I'd suspected in the back of my mind that they'd like Ivy, she's our kind of quirky.

Realising I haven't seen any of the others since coming through the door, I decide to have a look for the rest. I make a gesture to my group, towards the kitchen, then move to get another drink before I search for anyone.

This time, I grab a glass from a cupboard and mix myself a weak rum and coke from the plentiful bar available. I turn to inspect the room, quickly spotting Cara, who is holding court.

She's sat gracefully on a chair from the dining room table and is surrounded by a group of five guys and two girls who look enraptured by whatever she is saying. I make my way to them, standing on the outskirts of the group to hear what Cara's telling them. It turns out to be the story of a disastrous date involving a zoo break in. Looking at Cara I have no trouble believing it to be true. Half the group around me seem ready to break into a zoo for her.

As the story reaches its climax, with her date facing a rhino whose enclosure he'd fallen in, Cara spots me. She immediately stops her story and jumps up to hug me. While I hug her back, I watch the group disperse as though they have been dismissed.

I ask Cara if she is enjoying the party and am met with a pout as we both release the hug and she keeps a hold on my upper arms

"Boring, none of these people have anything interesting to say."

I laugh. "Have you considered letting them get a word in, to check that theory?" I'm pretty sure of the answer.

Cara tilts her head, pondering the idea. "What an interesting concept." She says, grinning mischievously.

I shake my head ruefully at her. "What about the others, where are they?"

She stops looking off into the distance, and her eyes spark with further amusement. "Well, Danny's over there." Cara points to the back-right corner of the room. I follow her finger with my eyes and see him standing there, intensely making out with my kind-of-friend Jackie. I grimace and make a mental note to give Jackie a talk on Monday on the importance of good taste. But for the moment, I just look away.

Cara laughs at the sight of my disgusted face, and continues, "And last I saw them, Lily and Sam were enjoying a moment alone in the back garden."

My eyebrows slowly rise as her words sink in. Ian's house doesn't have a back garden. As Cara continues to look at me with a satisfied smile on her face, it hits me. "They *made* a back garden?!" I exclaim. "Everyone knows there isn't a back garden. You're going to freak people out!" I am suddenly panicked.

Cara simply laughs again at my face and squeezes my arms. "Will, everyone is off their faces or soon to be. If they remember a garden tomorrow, they'll assume they're remembering wrong." She says with no edge of doubt in her voice. "Trust me, people believe they're mistaken or crazy, way before they believe in us."

It makes sense. I'd definitely jumped to the conclusion that I was crazy.

My breathing eases back to normal again, and Cara releases her hold on me. Everyone around us does seem to be moving in a way that suggests the room is spinning for them, they will probably discard the memory of a spinning garden tomorrow.

Before I can ask where Ella is, Cara answers me. "She's upstairs. On the landing."

I want to rush up the stairs immediately but hesitate, I don't want to just leave Cara. She notices the conflict on my face and defuses it.

"Just go. I'll wish Ian a happy birthday and blow his mind."

I'm not sure if blowing his mind refers simply to wishing him a happy birthday but decide I really don't want to clarify that and head off. The route to the bottom of the stairs is strewn with people, a few I stop to say hello to. British manners can be an obtrusive pain sometimes. It's only when I finally reach the steps that I allow myself to look up to the landing.

It acts like a balcony overlooking the ground floor. It only has three doors leading off from it, one to the bathroom, which unsurprisingly has a queue outside of it, one to Ian's room and a final one to his parent's room.

I climb the stairs while trying to both cherish my time reaching Ella, and get there as soon as possible. So, my body decides to move in a very stupid manner. My feet taking the stairs two at a time, while my legs themselves move slowly. It is ridiculous, but I forget about that when I reach the landing.

CHAPTER 8

Due to the brilliance of Ian's sound system, the music is only slightly less intense upstairs, but it's muted into soft background noise by Ella's presence.

Ella stands by the railing, which seems to be her comfortable position in life, and watches over the party, her face holding a mixture of emotions; amusement, sadness, guilt, curiosity and want. She doesn't look around when I reach her, but I feel sure she knows I'm here.

We survey the party together, in the peculiar situation of being both within and out-with the festivities. My eyes catch on Cara and Ian. I move my left hand along the bannister, resting it next to Ella's arms and pointing at the pair below.

"Look at that." I whisper.

Ella focusses her eyes on them too, and we watch the scene below play out.

I expected Ian to lose all semblance of cool with Cara, but as they speak, he looks quite measured. We see him nervously toy with the hair at the back of his neck while he talks and gestures to the dancing people. Cara must agree to dance with him, because she gives him her hand and they walk into the midst of the dancers. I see Ian use his free hand for a little fist pump, and smile to myself, happy for him.

They start dancing in the centre of the group, Cara swaying seductively while Ian uses very toned-down versions of his usual moves.

Glancing around the rest of the people, I find Ivy, still dancing with Jack, the pair of them have been joined by several more of my friends. Danny stands on the fringes of the group, dancing coolly and very close to Jackie, who seems to be enjoying herself. I also catch sight of Lily and Sam, apparently back from their garden, dancing sweetly just apart from the mosh pit of the rest.

I flick my gaze back to Ella, who is lost in the scene. "Do you want to join them?" I ask, as nervous as a preteen at their first school dance.

Ella turns to me, shocked, she moves away from the bannister in a stumble. "No, no I can't…I mean," Her eyes widen with fear of upsetting me. "I would but, I…don't know how to do *that*." She stammers, looking fearfully at the people below, like they are sharks waiting to bite.

I move away from the railing too and hold out my hands in a cautious open gesture. "That's ok. I just wondered if you'd like to." I'm stammering as well and curse myself for it. "I'm not very good at it either." I add, jokily, trying to lighten the topic.

Ella smiles gratefully at me, her whole posture relaxing. "I've never even tried to do it, the last time I went to one of these, it was still the fashion to waltz."

It takes a while for the words meaning to reach me. When were waltzes fashionable? I doubt that it's within my parent's lifetime, possibly my grandparents, I don't know.

I'd been so focussed on adjusting to the abilities that they all possessed that I'd lost sight of the other capacity of a God. Immortality. These people I'd come with to the party looked my age, but as evidenced by Ivy earlier that night, they can control those young appearances. For all I know they began, at the beginning.

I feel a creeping crawl over my skin as I look at Ella, taking in her possible age, taking in the possibilities of what they could all have lived through.

Though, as I look into her bright blue eyes, that peer back

at me anxiously, I realise that in this moment, it doesn't matter. This is a party and I am talking to a pretty girl, epiphanies can wait.

"We're even then. I've never tried to waltz." I say, dropping my hands that had remained raised and smiling at her. Smiling at this girl is truly the easiest thing to do.

"Do you want to?"

The words come as a total surprise. Ella says them with complete bravery.

She's asking me to dance.

I smile even wider, it's unbelievably easy to do with her. I hold out my hand. As I'd seen done in numerous cheesy films forced on me by my mum and Katie.

Ella takes my hand with a flourish matching the one I'd used and steps in closer to me.

Wordlessly, she moves my hand into position on her back, and places her hand on my shoulder. Guiding me with subtle pushes and pulls from her hands, we move together in the circle of a waltz. We move slowly, and I don't bother looking at my feet or counting in my head, I just look at her. Her face is lit from within by a humorous joy at taking an awkward me through the dance.

After a few circles, I attempt to spin Ella and because I catch her by surprise, she spins clumsily and falls back into me, laughing.

I hold her up and we stay there for a moment laughing together, until my phone buzzes.

We jump apart, I need to stop being shocked that my phone does anything around them. But my phone also needs to stop going off at the most annoying times.

I take my phone out, expecting a message from Ian saying something about dancing with Cara, or something else of equally no interest to me. Instead I read two words on the screen that makes my blood freeze in my veins.

Without hesitation, I take off down the stairs and push through people to the front door. My peripheral vision notes Ian being one of the people I pass but I don't stop. Shouts of my name erupt behind me as I go through the door.

I don't listen to them, well not until my feet suddenly stick to the grass beneath me.

"Will!"

I swivel in my glued position and move my head wildly between everyone that has followed me. Ella, Ian, Cara, Ivy, Lily and Sam all stand there, worried.

"What?!" I shout. "I have to go, I just…please." My hands pulling on my legs to get them to move away from their resolute position on the grass.

"Why, what happened? Talk to us." It's Cara's voice, sounding quite un-Cara like, with the sympathy etched into it.

The two words from the text are sprinting around my head, I can't get them out, but Ian gets there for me.

"It's Katie." He says, suddenly sober and sombre.

He's seen me like this once before. A few of my friends had been round at my house, roughly a year before, to do homework, I think. We'd heard loud coughing upstairs and I'd gone up to check it out. I'd found Katie coughing blood into the toilet, she was too small to reach the sink. Ian had been the one to stay and wait by my side for the ambulance, while I rubbed Katie's back and we spoke silly nonsense to her, to stop her being so scared.

That day, I'd been wild with worry too, that feeling never went away. The surge of needing to do something while fighting the desire to run away, it's inevitable with days and texts like those.

Before I manage a response, Danny emerges from the open doorway and stalks through the wall of the others. He grabs my arm and pulls me along with him, uprooting me with ease from the grass.

"I'll take you, wherever it is." He says it simply, clearly, no argument.

The shock of it being Danny to come to my aid doesn't even factor, I'm just relieved to be on my way to Katie.

"The hospital."

CHAPTER 9

We take the car from our drive to the party, and Danny gets us on our way to the hospital without any discussion. The only noise in the car comes from the erratic bouncing of my left knee. I can't sit still.

Eventually the silence becomes too much for me. "Why you?"

Danny sighs, and I see his hands tighten on the wheel. "I may not like you, but I've been there. You needed to go, and you didn't need them slowing you down with their concern."

The part about him not liking me comes as no surprise, though I don't know what his reasoning is. The fact he'd 'been there' does surprise me. The group of them seem pretty isolated from the rest of society in that big house, and I doubt they ever need to go to the hospital for themselves. Despite being curious about who he means, I don't ask, it's obviously personal and as stated, he doesn't like me.

I settle for saying, "Thank you." And then let the car lapse back into silence.

Danny isn't speeding exactly, he drives just on the edge of speeding, and weaves smoothly through the streets. I'm grateful for his efficient driving. I can't take any roadblocks just now.

I've only had one driving lesson in my life, and it was so far from smooth that my dad decided one was enough.

When we roll upfront of the hospital, I'm out the car before it has a chance to properly come to a halt. I don't know if Danny is going come after me, or if he's just acting as chauffeur, I just sprint away from him to reception.

Luckily, there's no queue to get to the desk, I'm not feeling very capable of patience right now.

"Katie Murphy." I say, practically collapsing onto the desk. "She's my sister. I heard she was brought in."

It's an elderly nurse sitting there, she must've seen hundreds or thousands of scared family members begging for news, but her eyes still feel for me as she looks up my sister. She must be a good nurse, the ones that care most always are.

"She was brought in after fainting at home. They think the faint was brought on by anaemia but are checking everything out. And they want to make sure she didn't hurt anything when she fell. She's up in the paediatric ward."

I know exactly where the paediatric ward is, and head off towards it after offering a quick, sincere thanks to the nurse.

Out the corner of my eye I see Danny strolling behind me as I walk, I can't be bothered enough to tell him to leave or to want him to leave, so I ignore him.

The ward is only one floor up, so we reach its doors quickly and I see my mum instantly through them, wringing her hands and wearing pyjamas.

I fly through the doors and hug her. At just over six foot, I completely tower over her five-foot five figure, which normally bothers her, but in situations like this, when I can smother her in a hug, she doesn't mind. She clings to me, her body shaking.

My dad stands a few paces behind my mum, and when I catch his eye over her shoulders, he explains what happened.

"They think she's been skipping her iron supplement. Might've had a bad head rush standing up and just fallen over. Looks like she didn't hurt herself when she fell."

I close my eyes in relief, she's ok, she'll be ok. My arms

fall away from my mum and I take a few steps towards my dad, looking into the open room he stands beside.

Katie lays in a bed too big for her small frame. Her eyes are closed in imitation of sleep, but I know well enough that she's faking.

I enter the room and walk swiftly over to her, bending down to whisper in her ear, "Scooch, Kid."

Her little face smiles, eyes still closed, and she weakly shuffles over a bit. I bound into the open space around her, curling my long legs up in all the unused space at the bottom of the bed.

"So, tablet skipping huh?" I say, tutting as I do, keeping my tone light. Only way to do serious with a six-year-old is to be very unserious yourself.

"They said those ones were to make me stronger, but I felt strong anyway." Katie whispers to me, whispering because it's a secret, and we can always tell each other secrets.

"You felt strong because of the tablets." I say, gently urging her towards understanding.

"You don't think I'm strong?" Asks Katie, staring at me with large eyes.

My heart breaks looking into those eyes, the eyes of the kid who never wanted to be a princess in any story I told, only a knight, who protected everyone from everything. "You're the strongest person I know." I whisper back, trying not to let my voice crack, or the tears swimming in my eyes fall.

We stare at each other, no words, faces totally open. Moments later, Katie nods her head at me, and I know she'll take all her tablets from now on. Though our mum will leave no room for doubt from now on.

With the serious bit over, I decide to share another secret between us. "So, there's this girl…" I begin.

Katie squeals immediately and claps her hands twice before clapping them to her face, the picture of glee. I chuckle at the reaction and open my mouth to elaborate. Ready to start by trying to put into words, those beautiful blue eyes of Ella's, but we are interrupted.

"Will, we need to let Katie sleep and get her energy back." Comes my mum's voice, behind me.

"Mu-um!" Katie and my voices chant, in the moaning way only little kids do. We were just getting to the good bit.

I turn and see my mum's no-nonsense face and don't fight. I kiss the side of Katie's head, then clamber off the bed and kiss my mum's temple, as well, on my way out.

I know my mum needs help with Katie, but she has my dad, and Katie needs help being allowed to be a little kid, what else are siblings for.

Back in the corridor, my dad is muttering to a doctor and Danny is leaning, coolly, against a wall. I walk over to him.

"She's ok."

Danny nods. "I know. I've been eavesdropping."

Part of me wants to guffaw at how open he is about listening in, but I don't bother. "Why did you stay?" I ask, the behaviour of this guy is a mystery to me.

"The others like you, they'll probably not want me to leave you alone." I want to point out that my parents are here, but since my dad is busy taking up the doctor's time and my mum is still in Katie's room probably keeping her awake by obsessively straightening her sheets to help her sleep, I don't really have an argument.

I settle for slumping against the wall next to Danny relaxing into the silence he offers.

In the end, my parents don't feel like they can leave and have cots set up in Katie's room, to stay the night. They worry for a while about how I'll get home, since it's nearing 2am, but Danny says he'll give me another lift.

On our way out, my dad slips Danny a twenty in thanks,

which he takes, but I see him drop it into the first charity collection box we pass.

When we reach the parking lot again, they're all stood there, resting by the car. The five others like Danny, and Ian. I stare at him in particular as we head towards the car.

"I know I'm a bad host." He says, jovially, taking a few steps to meet me in a bro-hug.

"She's ok." I whisper in his ear, causing Ian to give me a tight squeeze before releasing the hug, eyes shining with relief.

"How'd you get here?" I hear Danny ask from behind me.

"Bus." Supplies Ivy.

I turn to look at Cara, one eyebrow cocked in surprise. I thought she didn't do buses.

Her face looks between me and Danny, mock shocked. "One car ride together, and you two become twins." She says.

I glanced over to Danny and see he's been making the same face I have. Sufficiently creeped out, I turn away from him abruptly. Which causes everyone to laugh, I assume that again, Danny and I had matching reactions.

Ian doesn't want to go back to his party, "They'll finish it without me, I can just go back and assess the damage tomorrow. I'm here."

I appreciate the gesture, but don't feel too bad about Ian's sacrifice, not when Cara is smiling at him the way she is.

We all agree to go back to mine for an impromptu supportive sleep over. Lily doesn't want to leave me alone, and Ivy is very excited at the prospect of seeing my house. Which I find both sweet and strange but shrug it off.

We all lumber into the car, which had become so spacious earlier that it doesn't need to stretch for Ian, who sits himself in between Ivy and Cara. The back of my mind is curious about whether Ian has noticed anything strange about the group we're keeping company with, but most of me is still in a state of relief about Katie.

I lean my head back in the seat with my eyes closed, tired after all the nerves finish running through my body. Suddenly I feel completely alive again, Ella has placed her hand over mine, in the space between us, and lightly squeezed. It feels like a crushing of my whole chest, but totally exhilarating.

I fight not to move in my seat and react for the whole car to see. The only move I make is to bring my thumb round and back over one of Ella's fingers and return the squeeze. After a few minutes, I open my eyes realising I haven't given Danny who is driving again, my address.

"Wait, I thought we were going to mine?" I say, swivelling to look back over at our driver. Worrying for a moment, he's taking me, but more importantly Ian, to their house.

"We are." He states, simply.

"But I didn't give you my address."

"And?" He asks, never taking his eyes off the road as he takes a turn, a correct turn.

I shake my head disbelievingly and return to sitting normally in my chair, going over the possible ways he might know where I live and coming up blank. Glancing over at Ian to check if he's noticed anything, I see I have no reason to worry. He's telling Ivy and Cara the story of when me and him had gone on a bike race through town with Felix, and how he'd ended up breaking his collarbone.

Ivy is laughing at the story and interjecting cycling mishaps of her own, while Cara simply listens in. It's nice to see the two girls not clash, and to see that Ian isn't giving all his attention to just Cara. The spark of a good friendship looks like it's kindling between him and Ivy, which I approve of resolutely.

Sam and Lily are talking amongst themselves, well Lily is talking to Sam who seems to literally never speak. While I spoke to Danny, Ella had looked around with me and is now talking with Lily. They're discussing the party and all the silly behaviour they'd witnessed, while giggling sweetly.

I take the opportunity to look at Ella for a moment, trying to put straight in my head what looking at her does to me, but I can't make sense of it. It's like a feeling in my entire being that English, has, not yet, been able to properly define in its long history. Blinking to bring myself back to the car, I join in Lily and Ella's conversation, supplying names for the dances they're describing to each other. Ella lets out a guffaw at the sound of one dance, and Ian offers to teach them how to do it back at mine. Which Ivy instantly agrees to.

"You know what? How about we break out the 'Just Dance' back at yours? Always hilarious." Ian suggests.

I laugh and nod, liking the sound of that, but the noise comes out sounding oddly hollow in the suddenly silent car.

Me and Ian look between all the others, who are blankly glancing between each other. I flash back to Ella telling me about waltzing being her last dancing experience, and it dawns on me that with the possible age and seclusion of them all, video games could be pretty alien.

"None of you have ever played it??" Asks Ian, totally incredulous.

"We'll teach you." I say, smiling around at them all. Letting my gaze rest on Ella for slightly longer than the others and giving another squeeze to her fingers, which I still hold. She is back to having that scared look on her face from the party, but tries to smile.

Her face relaxes after another moment and Lily pipes up from the front, "Sounds fun." Ivy nods her head, and Cara begrudgingly agrees as well. Sam says nothing, but I assume Lily was speaking for both of them.

When we draw up to my house, I just stare at it, strangely afraid, until Ian claps me on the shoulders.

"Come on dude, 'Just Dance'."

I laugh and get out the car with him, remembering at the last moment to hold the door open for the girls. Cara pats my cheek on her way out, making my eyes roll. As I approach the door to unlock my house for everyone, I feel cautious for them judging it. I was bad enough the first time Ian saw my house, it's a lot smaller than his, which means it's a dog house compared to the others' place.

I try not to care though, remembering that apart from Danny, and occasionally Cara, they are all very nice people. My thoughts snag a little calling them 'people', but I shove it aside as unimportant for the moment.

CHAPTER 10

As soon as I unlock the door, Ivy starts running around like a puppy. I gesture everyone else into the living room. Before sitting down, Cara asks where the bathroom is. I hadn't expected her or any of them to ask that. In the back of my mind I was working under the assumption they didn't need to do any of those pesky human things like eating, sleeping or using the bathroom.

"You need to use it?" I ask, stupidly.

Behind Cara I see Ian giving me a very perplexed look, showing he thinks I'm crazy. Cara herself just smiles at me sweetly instead of answering. I shake my head at myself. "Right, sorry. Upstairs, first on your left."

Cara leaves to follow my instructions, and Ian continues staring at me, confused. I am happily distracted by Lily pointing at the tv, which has our old Wii next to it, with the box for 'Just Dance' resting on top of it. It's the only game we ever play. She looks dubious, when she asks. "Is it this we're playing?"

Everyone else looks around at me curiously, except for Danny, who stands in the corner of the room inspecting family photos on a bookshelf. "Yeah, it's a video game." I say, moving forward to set it up.

Ivy bounces back into the room just then and offers a great distraction, stating loudly, "I love your house!"

I turn away from the game set up to smile at her. "Thanks."

She grins at me and flops onto a sofa, hugging her knees looking very content. "It's just so homey."

"It sure is." Comes Danny's disdainful voice from the edge of the room, not looking away from the bookcase.

"Aw don't be jealous Dan." Cara reappears in the doorway as she says it and stares at Danny teasingly.

He glares at her and silence falls in the room. I busy myself with the game, checking the batteries of the controllers. My mind is buzzing over Cara's choice of words. Jealous? Why jealous? Then I remember Danny saying on the way to the hospital about having 'been there' and I let myself wonder for a second or third time that night, what these people have lived through. Trying to defuse the tension however, I hop off the train of thought I've been on and turn to face the room, holding up four controllers.

"Who wants to play?"

Ian and Ivy jump up immediately and grab a controller each. He begins explaining the premise of the game to her. Lily comes up beside me and takes another controller, I wonder as she does, how her style of dancing will translate to the oddness of the game's moves. Cara pushes herself away from the door frame and takes the final one.

The four of them begin flicking through songs, arguing about which one to do, apart from Lily who doesn't seem to have heard of any of them. Sam sits on the sofa and amusedly watches them all, while Danny continues to glare at Cara's back. While looking around at them all, I realise Ella is nowhere to be seen.

I exit the living room to find her, sure I'll miss some of the hilarity that is bound to unravel. Heading upstairs I quickly find Ella. She's standing in Katie's room, holding up Winston, the toy dog, and inspecting his cute face. As I enter the room, Ella quickly puts him back down.

"Sorry, I shouldn't be here." She starts scanning the floor as though she's lost something in it, but I am quite sure she hasn't.

"It's okay." I say, gently.

"No, it's…I'm not good with this. I'm not good around normal." She tries to explain, her blue eyes taking in the pink little girls' room, in the average house.

Most of my life, up until meeting them all, has been pretty normal. My family is a mum and a dad with a son and a daughter. Even Katie, what happened, was happening, to her, is fairly unextraordinary. It's the only unextraordinary thing about her. Then I remember all the little details of my life. The ridiculous dance routine me and my friends made up when we were eight, leading to my parents buying 'Just Dance' in the first place. The time Katie and I experimented with a brownie recipe adding every sugary sweet we had in the kitchen to it and giving ourselves the best/worst sugar rushes alive. The whole month when I was younger, before Katie was born, that who did the dishes was decided by a race to the lamppost at the end of our street, by me, my mum and my dad, who always lost.

I smile at all those memories and look into Ella's eyes. "You know, the most normal thing in the world is to be a little strange. You seem right on track." While my words are still sinking in, I turn to go back downstairs.

Ella catches me on the landing. "You think I'm strange." Her voice is tinged with worry, and it is the cutest thing.

I bend my head down, so it's close to her height, and sincerely say. "I like that you're strange." Trying to get across with my tone, exactly which kind of 'like' I mean.

Ella smiles at me, warmly, and suddenly seems a lot closer than she had before. We begin to move ever so slowly towards each other, but just then.

"Booyah! Cara you suck!"

Ivy's shout comes from downstairs, and the moment is broken.

Without saying anything, Ella and I start downstairs to

see what has happened, we walk into a hilarious scene, even Danny is smiling.

Ian is doubled up laughing, while Ivy does the most enthusiastic victory dance I've ever seen, and Cara stands with one hand on her hip, looking unamused.

The scores flash on the screen, showing that player 2, who I assume is Ivy, has won, with players 1 and 3 a bit behind and then player 4 with barely any points. I catch Ian's eye as his breathing stabilises after all the laughing.

"Who were you?" I ask, nudging my head at the screen.

"Player 2."

My eyebrows furrow in confusion as I turned to look at Ivy and her ongoing victory dance.

"She was player 1." Supplies Ian, amused.

I glance at the screen again before exclaiming, "You came third?!"

Ivy pauses her dance and looks at me. "Yeah, but I beat her." She replies, pointing at Cara.

We all burst out laughing.

"You weren't even doing the right moves." Says Ian.

"Mine were better." Says Cara assuredly. Making us all laugh harder. Cara's eyes flash a little at us all, and she tosses her controller to me. "See if you can do better."

Lily passes her controller to Sam, Ivy to Ella, and Ian very hesitantly holds his out to Danny, who stares him down, arms crossed. Ian relents and moves to play another round but Danny's face breaks into a reluctant smile, and he takes the controller, clapping Ian's back as he does.

Ella is then player 1 and has to scroll through the song options. Ivy and Ian shout out their choices, and Ella picks the first one she comes to. As the song loads up, I find Ella's gaze, trying to ask without words if she wants to do this.

She smiles back at me and whispers, "Well, you tried waltzing tonight." I grin back.

Out the corner of my eye I see Sam and Danny play fight, elbowing each other and laughing. For the first time since meeting him, Danny seems relaxed and young.

The song starts and none of us are the picture of elegance in following the moves. Sam and I fumble along, a bit robotically, Danny is too cool to do the big moves so does everything half-heartedly, and Ella does pretty well, except she keeps bursting into laughter and missing stuff.

We play for several more songs, mixing up who plays against who, and get to witness another victory dance of Ivy's. We only stop playing when Ian falls asleep on the sofa and we realise it's nearing five in the morning.

I gather blankets and sleeping bags into the living room, and everyone happily arranges themselves sleepover style on the floor, except Danny, who leaves to sleep in my parents' room, ignoring my protests not to do so, and Cara, who asks if she can sleep in my room. I agree as I can in no way imagine her consenting to sleep on the floor.

After lying down, the tiredness hits everyone and talking ceases. I was wrong in my assumption these Gods didn't need sleep.

As I drift off it truly hits me, that the people I am surrounded by, have, over the course of just a few days, become friends of mine. And in the moment right before my mind switches off, I also realise that I still know next to nothing about them.

CHAPTER 11

It's my parents arriving home that wakes me up. I blink the sleep out of my eyes and see that Ian and I are alone in the living room.

My dad walks in, and while taking off his coat grumbles to us, "You could've slept on the sofas you know?"

Ian and I don't say anything; he looks just as confused as I am by the disappearance of our friends.

My dad leaves the room again, and we hear him speaking in the hallway, we also hear the unmistakeable noise of a certain little girl.

I scramble to my feet, forgetting the others and run to see Katie. She squeals when I get into the hallway and hugs my knees like always. Ian follows behind me and, after catching sight of him Katie calls, "Uncle Ian!" She's called him that forever. We don't know how she'd come to the 'uncle' assumption, but Ian always wore it with pride.

"Hey Katie, hey sis." He adds, directing it to my mum, his little joke based off the uncle title that only he and Katie find funny.

My mum rolls her eyes as she always does to Ian and asks us all for breakfast orders. Pancakes are quickly demanded, with Katie insisting on assisting.

The rest of us start to head back to the living room to wait for food, but I excuse myself to go to the bathroom.

Upstairs, I check on mine and my parents' rooms, to see if Cara and Danny have left too. They have, after making the beds, from the pristine look of them. I also see that all the blankets and sleeping bags from the night before have been folded and packed away, placed neatly at the bottom of my bed.

Slightly confused by the organised early departure of everyone, I turn to go to the bathroom but notice a piece of paper propped up against a book on the small desk of my room.

I can be a bit of a neat freak about my room so never leave paper lying out. I double back and pick up the piece of paper, smiling down at the words on it.

'I don't have many days out of the house. Thank you for that one. It was wonderful, probably because it was a little bit strange. Ella'

The handwriting is a swooping cursive, and the note itself a great gift, I don't want to put it down. After carefully folding it inside my wallet, I go brush my teeth in the bathroom, humming as I do.

Ian has been coming round to my house for over a decade, but he somehow still feels awkward around my dad. My dad is by no means warm and cuddly, he's the kind of parent that is just always there. He's present in my life but not that active in it. It means that while I love him as part of my family, I'm pretty neutral to him as a person, I'm certainly not scared of him, like Ian is.

When I go back downstairs and join the two of them, I am joining complete silence. My dad has picked up a book and started reading it to casually fill time before breakfast, while Ian sits abnormally upright and still, staring at a point on the wall.

Flopping down next to him, I lightly kick his knee to get to get him to look at me and then raise my hands and gave him a 'what are you doing?' expression. He shrugs, looking just as confused by his own behaviour, which makes me laugh so hard I bury my face in a cushion, causing my dad to look up at us, slightly concerned.

Most of the reason my dad doesn't talk to Ian is because Ian doesn't talk to him, he talks to my other friends just fine. I'm pretty sure when my dad got on social media, it was Felix who explained to him how to use it without being a cliché annoying parent.

We are saved from the silence by my mum calling that food is ready, and we all jump up to collect it. My mum is a modern woman, she'll make us food because she likes to cook, and my dad is awful, but she draws the line at catering to us in our seats.

Katie has busied herself drawing faces on the pancakes with various toppings and dictates which plate belongs to who. I get a blueberry smiley face, Ian a chocolate smiley face with strawberry ears on the side (he has slightly large ears which can only be commented on by Katie who loves their goofy quality), my dad is handed a pancake with jam smudges done in resemblance to his scruffy beard.

We all take our plates happily, complimenting Katie's artistic prowess. My dad sneaks a knife out the kitchen, so he can spread the jam over the whole pancake but is careful not to be caught.

"That boy was nice to drive you home last night, who is he again?" Asks my dad, when we are all sat back down. I know he's using 'again' just in case Danny is a regular figure in my life that he's blanked on until now.

Surprisingly it's Ian who answers my dad. "That was Danny, one of Wills' *many* new friends."

His words come as a surprise to me, Ian had hung out with everyone seamlessly last night, it hadn't really struck me that apart from Cara he hadn't seen any of them before, or heard about any of them.

"New friends?" Asks my mum, joining us with a pancake of her own that holds a resemblance to her through a whipped cream hair style. Despite my being nineteen and having developed adequate to good social skills, she still worries about me having enough friends.

"They're friends of Cara's, I met them when we were working together at hers. They're nice." I say to them all defensively, before shoving some pancake in my mouth, in an effort to avoid answering more questions about them. I want to limit the amount of lying I have to do.

"One of them seems especially nice to Will." Says Ian, looking down at his plate while smirking. I glare over at him, guessing immediately at what he is insinuating.

"Really?" Says my mum, eyes shining.

"Really." Replies Ian, nodding at her expression.

"Oh, Will that's so exciting."

I choke a little on my pancake, not enjoying my mother's condescension, however well it is intended. While I'm still getting my act together, my dad chimes in.

"Are you planning on treating this girl properly?"

Ian bursts out laughing, before quickly trying to smother it for fear of my dad. I meanwhile open my mouth to splutter something, I don't know what, but am stopped in my tracks by mum hissing at him, "Ian never said it was a girl." She cuts me a loving eye after saying it to show she is accepting of whatever, and despite me again approving of the gesture, I want the madness of this conversation to end.

Unluckily, this is when Katie enters the room, her own pancake not even visible under all the sugary stuff crammed on top of the plate, in a mound.

"I thought you were going to tell me about the girl first." She huffs, literally stomping her foot as she does.

I turn all my attention to Katie, an apology written all over my face. She has dibs on hearing things from me first.

My mum interrupts the silence that is forming and swoops in to take Katie's plate, as much as she might want to treat Katie the day after a hospital visit, my mum can't allow her to eat junk like that. They head to the kitchen to rearrange the plate with a lot healthier stuff, arguing with each other on the way, my dad grumbles out of his seat and goes to mediate, meaning he goes to agree with his wife.

Once we are alone, I turn back to Ian and glare at him again, talking about girls in front of parents is definitely against the friend code. He stands his ground though.

"I just wanted to get something out of you. You never talk about this stuff and you treated last night as so normal with them."

"I thought you liked them."

"I did, I do. They were cool people, apart from Danny, I don't get him. I'm just confused about what was going on."

"Then you could've asked me."

"You would've brushed me off, like always."

I don't have a comeback for that, the 'like always' stings. I admit I'm not always an open book, some paragraphs or pages or chapters of my life are blacked out or written in code, not for others to see, but I hadn't thought that Ian or anyone else noticed. I breathe hard out my nose and relent.

"I should've mentioned them before I showed up to a party with them." After I say it, Ian is still looking at me expectantly. "What?" I ask.

He rolls his eyes like I should know precisely what. "Ella. I want you to tell me what's going on there."

My cheeks flush, and I curse them for it. I have no idea what is going on there. I know the basics, I like her, but that's the only thing clear enough for me to explain, and Ian seems to be expecting a lot more.

We are interrupted by my family returning, with Katie now holding a plate lumbered with a lot of fruit, but an extra pancake, a sad compromise but one nonetheless. Wanting both to avoid the return of the girl conversation with my parents, and to not leave Ian hanging, I suggest me and him eat with Katie outside for some fresh air. Fresh air is the trick to getting my mum to let you do anything, she thinks fresh air will help everything, so always agrees.

The three of us carry our plates outside and sit down in the middle of the pitiful grassy area in our small, almost dead garden. The space is only used for hanging laundry most of the time, so never looks that nice, but under the sunny blue sky of the day, it's passable.

As soon as we are all settled, the pair of them turn to me with the same questioning eyes. I swear that sometimes Ian is just as much Katie's brother as I am, they're so in sync.

I open my mouth to try to explain, but come up short, Ian takes pity on me. "Tell us like it's a bedtime story for Katie." I don't know why Ian suggests doing it like that until he speaks his next words to usher me along. "You're only good at being honest when you're being fake, dude."

The words take a few moments to sink in, and at first, I feel that I should be offended but I realise it's true. I spend so much of my time living in a dream, telling Katie stories concocted from a parallel version of my life, listening to other people's music instead of listening to my own thoughts and reading books instead of my textbooks. I like stories.

Maybe that's why I can just about deal with learning what Cara and Ella and all the others are, they're just another fiction to add to the list I live in.

I smile to myself and begin. "I met her from afar, it was only a glimpse not even an introduction, but it felt like something, some big beginning. Then a few days later I saw her properly, again from a distance but was probably for the best, up close too soon, might've killed me. She is beautiful, in every way, especially her eyes, they're so blue you want to jump in them and swim. That's it, that's why she's so intriguing, she invites you in to get to know her, because you know it'll be good, whatever it is. I still don't know her, but it feels like experiencing her is enough, watching the way she watches the world, helping her be less afraid of it. Being something she's not afraid of, it's the best thing I've ever done."

I bring myself to a pause then, having to stop speaking because I am getting way too carried away, I'm rambling like an idiot, saying things that don't really make sense. But when I look back at Ian and Katie, they don't seem to think that, Katie is smiling at me with her face shining, and Ian is shaking his head slightly, astounded.

"Sounds wonderful."

The voice comes from behind me and we all turn to look at the back door. My dad is stood there, leaning against the doorframe, legs crossed over slightly, his face strange. I try to find the word for it, and after a second of staring into his face, it hits me, he looks proud.

I wonder if he's about to ask if I'll treat her right again, but he doesn't. He turns and goes back into the house, whistling as he does. My dad never whistles.

"It does you know." Says Ian, in a whisper as my dad retreats into the house.

I smile to myself again as I come to a decision in my mind. "It is."

CHAPTER 12

I spend the rest of the day with my family. Ian leaves early enough to avoid joining in on game night. Monopoly is dangerous with my mum, she gets competitive and forgets to be the caring one in the family for a few hours, every time we play.

I arrive back at my flat really late that night but am still there by the time my partier flatmate, Isaac, is heading out. We bump into each other in the kitchen and have a quick catch up, which consists mostly of him joking that I'm out more than him lately, making me laugh as I can't disagree.

Lying down on my bed, I toss and turn for a long time, manipulating the pillows into all kinds of positions to try and get comfortable, but the mounting stress in my stomach makes that an impossibility. I have big plans for Monday, which makes the day seem altogether too close and too distant.

I mean, I've never asked anyone out before, so I can't blame myself for being terrified, and she isn't just anyone. she is a practically literal God, she's Ella.

It's only on Monday morning, when I wake up from my half-hearted sleep, that I realise I don't have a phone number or any other way of contacting Cara, or the others. I wanted to text one of them for advice on asking Ella out.

I pull up Facebook to look her up, I don't even have her as a friend on that. I've got everyone on Facebook, everyone does. They aren't everyone, I guess. Ian and Jackie had had a week where they competed to see who could friend as many random as possible on nights out. Jackie had won, but quickly deleted them all to avoid creepy messages. I realise as well that I don't have Cara's last name, or know if any of them even have last names, so I give up.

My Monday timetable doesn't include any English classes, so I can't be sure I'll see Cara, but I hope anyway. My chicken heart needs girl advice, well specifically Girl-God advice. Calling Ella, a goddess, even in my head, sounds like way too much. I'm also still on the fence about calling them Gods at all, I haven't gotten enough details, our conversations had descended into being friendly over inquisitive.

Isaac is leaving for class at the same time I'm heading out for philosophy, so we head to campus together. I am never not amazed by Isaac's ability to make it to class, even when royally hungover, but I'm not as impressed by his hangover cure. A smoothie made of yoghurt and banana with sweet chili sauce blended in, the thought of the final ingredient always makes me gag.

In the walk to class Isaac fills me in on the events of his night out. He'd apparently been a second away from having something happen with a guy from his psychology class he liked, but they'd been interrupted by a girl, a very drunk girl, going over to them and flirting with each in turn. I laugh along with Isaac's impression of the girl and wonder for a moment about asking for his help with Ella, but we aren't really those kinds of friends.

Isaac abandons me when he reaches campus, he sees the guy from his class heading to their building and doesn't want him to think we're 'together'. He mutters something about 'gay guy problems' before jogging off.

I turn towards my lecture building but look back just in time to see Isaac hold the door open for his crush with a sweeping gesture, and them laughing together. I smile, happy for them, but feel a tug in my chest, guiltily sad it isn't me having a cute moment like that, something so easy.

Ian has already taken his seat when I arrive, he holds up his hand to make sure I see him, and I make my way over. When I take my seat, Ian immediately leans in next to me.

"So?"

I told him before he left my house that I wanted to do something about liking Ella, he apparently thought I'd act fast about it.

"Not seen her yet. Kind of want to talk to Cara first, see if there's any history I need to know about."

"Why don't you ask Ivy? She's joining us for lunch."

My eyebrows knit together in confusion, in place of actually asking how that was happening.

Ian jerks his thumb towards Jack, sitting on his other side. "We invited her on Saturday."

Jack tunes into the conversation and leans forward to see me properly. "Yeah." Jack is a man of few words.

I grin at them, pleased they liked her. Ivy is very cool. "Okay great, I'll check with her about it then."

Just then our lecturer rushes in, dumping his bag next to the computer at the front before immediately starting to speak. He has a habit of doing that, which means he always rushes through the first half of his lectures, despite just arriving two minutes late, and we're all forced to take hurried notes. I still like this lecturer though, he uses helpful metaphors.

He spends the hour discussing where ourselves begins and ends, and I find myself distracted by comparing the ideas to the others I was getting to know.

Ian and jack run off to another class but I head straight to the canteen to hang around until lunch. I sit with an increasingly cold coffee, mulling over the lecturer's words. Deciding I need to ask a hell of a lot more questions about who these new friends of mine are. While being careful to keep in mind they are my friends, except Danny.

I'm jerked away from my thoughts by someone chucking themselves into the seat next to me, luckily it's bolted down, or it would've flown across the hall.

It's Ivy, looking the same as she had at the party physically, but wearing dark green corduroy dungarees and a loose plain white t shirt, looking like an art student. She puts her feet up on the seat, and curls herself up, smiling at me. "Surprise!"

"You always are."

"A compliment I'm sure."

We continue grinning at each other. I always feel so at ease with Ivy, there is an aura of breeziness around her at all times. "Glad Ian and Jack invited you along."

"Me too. They're nice guys."

I find it oddly funny she referred to them as 'nice' when Ian called her 'cool' but neither were wrong.

"Can I ask you a possibly awkward question?" I ask, glancing surreptitiously around the room to make sure it's just her I was speaking to.

"Yeah, course." Says Ivy, smile turning warmer.

"Would it be crazy if I asked out Ella?" My words come out in a nervous rush, and I toy roughly with the hair on the back of my neck.

Ivy's jade green eyes look at me, through me, more seriously than I thought the girl capable. I want to go back on the question immediately, not hear the answer those serious eyes seem to foretell.

"It's complicated." Begins Ivy, saying the words carefully, as though laying out each syllable before me to make sure I understand.

"I know it wouldn't be uncomplicated, but would it really be so bad?" I ask, my voice turning slightly whiney, which I hate myself for instantly.

She closes her eyes, looking like she is having to stomp

down images or memories brought forward by my question, which solidifies the great unease I am feeling, and adding guilt to it. A long pause lingers between us; I hadn't thought such quiet was possible around Ivy.

"You're only just getting to know us, Will. We've all got a long history, and that comes with a lot of drama, for all of us, Ella especially. You two do seem to be getting along well, which is great for her, but you might need a little more time to know what you're ready to deal with."

Ella doesn't seem like something I would have to 'deal with', but I get what Ivy means, kind of. You might not need to know someone's history in order to be their friend, but it's more necessary when contemplating something more.

I nod at Ivy, showing I'm taking in her words and accepting them, she holds my shoulder for a moment before shoving it around playfully, easing us back into our normal laid-back way of interacting.

It strikes me as Ian, Jack and a few others begin grabbing the seats around us, how quickly Ivy can go from acknowledging the fact she has had a much longer and more dramatic past than I or anyone else here had had, to acting just like the rest of my friends, light and full of youthful vibrance. As I watch her joke with Ian about his woeful dancing skills, I wonder how much of it is real, hoping it's everything.

Ian notices me going into reflective mode and, acting as the good friend he is, throws a piece of his roll at me to bring me out of the depths of my own head. I snap back into place and throw the roll back at him, leading us all into a miniature food fight, that lasts about thirty seconds before Jackie points out we are idiots, causing us to aim at her, using up all our ammo.

She huffily brushes the crumbs of her jumper and scoops them onto the table, refusing to put it on the floor and add to the cleaner's work. Then Jackie fixes her gaze on Ivy, one of only two other girls at our table and a new face, obviously trying to change the topic away from food and our idiocy. "You were at Ian's party, right?"

"Yeah, Will invited me." Ivy gives me a side smile, which I return, I'm a little surprised Jackie remembers Ivy since she seemed taken up with Danny at the party.

"Will invited a lot of people." Adds Ian, not sounding annoyed at all. I think he's gotten used to the fact I'd brought the others but notice that he's using the point to hint towards Danny's attendance. I love how his mind works.

As we are a group of friends made up majorly by guys, we sometimes go along a bit too much with stereotypes and are protective of the girls when it comes to boys, especially with Jackie, she has proven to have some iffy taste.

"Yeah, you seemed to spend some time with one of them." Says Jack, we are all definitely aiming the conversation in the same direction.

Those of us that are facing Jackie's side of the table begin leaning in, attempting to look worthy of her confidence. Jackie picks up on what we are doing pretty quickly and rolls her eyes, beginning to shake her head, making her curls of black hair bounce around her.

Surprisingly Ivy joins in before we can say anymore, "Oh you were the one with Danny! Fun, isn't he?" She asks, picking up Ian's coffee cup to steal a sip, glancing over the cup for the other girl's reaction.

There's a knowing, suggestive tone in her voice that shocks me, making me blurt out. "Aw don't talk about him like that. Isn't he like your brother?"

Ivy chokes on her sip of coffee, full on chokes. Ian slaps her on the back trying to help and we all stiffen in the way you do when you feel like you should be helping but there's nothing for you to do. After the coughing subsides, Ivy is just laughing. "No, he's nothing like my brother. We go back a long way but just...no."

I feel stupid for assuming, they all live together but that doesn't make them family. Apart from Lily and Sam I don't really know much about the relationships between the others. I hold up my hands in apology and surrender. Ivy accepts the gesture and claps me on the shoulder again.

Possibly to try to get us all away from the awkwardness of the choking episode, or to stop everyone looking at Ivy, Jackie starts talking. "Whoever he is, he is fun to party with. He does go a bit far with the dark and mysterious thing though, I couldn't get a straight answer about anything from him."

It isn't the first time Jackie's described a guy like that, it's her type, she likes working people out and normally gives up on them once she has, or once she figures she isn't going to be able to. Ivy nods along, understanding completely.

"Yeah, he is a fan of that archetype. Don't take it personally."

As Ivy speaks, I realise Ian's hand is still on her back after slapping it earlier, and she is leaning back into it comfortably.

I decide I'm going to have to talk about that with Ian at some point, I haven't had an update on girls from him since his crush on with Cara. But it looks like he's changed his Godly interest.

The rest of our time is spent catching up on all the stories from the party, and showing off pictures from the night, most of which are fuzzy ones, taken from the dance. No one mentions the fact that me and Ian disappeared early in the night, but we do find out that the fun only wrapped up at around six, when the sun was coming up and the booze had run out.

I don't have any classes for the rest of the day so am planning on heading back to my flat and catching up on some of the work I haven't been doing due to the whirlwind of new people I was hanging out with. I excuse myself from the group at the same time as with Ivy, who is going to meet

Cara for some shopping, which she announces with an obvious grimace.

As we head away from the others, I'm not quite sure what to say to Ivy, thinking I should probably make sure she knows I have taken in what we'd spoken about before, but mostly wanting to stay in the bubble of ignoring it we'd been in with the others. Ivy decides for me.

"You should come round later, learn about some of our history."

My stomach knots with apprehension, knowing that this is the what I really needed to know about, in order to find out what I'd been most curious about when I met them. But I'm torn by the fact that finding out might ruin the friendships I was making with them. I'm worried that they might turn from people in my eyes to Gods.

Whether that change would be good or bad, I really don't know.

CHAPTER 13

I get some reading done back at my flat, all while tapping my fingers furiously and unconsciously on the desk next to me. If Ian was with me, I feel like I would've had my hand broken. I'm not sure how much time to leave before I head to Ivy's, but I feel like it should be a couple hours minimum. It doesn't seem likely that Cara would shop quickly, no matter how much Ivy might want to. All the reading I'm doing is going right over my head though, the words are being glanced at but not seen, and the sentences as a whole are a complete blur.

There is noise coming from my kitchen, and I debate for a moment going through to check out who it is. If it's Isaac I could ask about the guy in his class, if it's Eric, my other, far quieter, flat mate, I could have small talk about our classes before one of us eventually leaves in silence, it's always a tossup which one of us does it. The otherwise silence in my room is collapsing in on me, and seems to physically push me out of my seat.

I go through to the kitchen. Luckily, it is Isaac in there, I do like Eric but in the recent days I've felt the need for Isaac's company a lot more, he is a good distraction. Everything about Isaac is distracting, even the way he cooks. Nothing stays in the same place for more than a few seconds, pots are shifted around as he checks on them, and ingredients are constantly being picked up as he considers adding more of them or putting them away if he is done. It's a whole show, I've always respected it, he makes cooking a performance, I just make pasta and stand flicking through my phone while it boils. Isaac lives in everything he does.

He notices me as he jumps around the room, even Isaac himself doesn't stay still, he is always moving as though he has to show how lanky and flimsy he is at all times. It also makes his blond hair flop around his head, which I'd always considered a way of making him seem cute to guys, which in fairness works well, but also works on girls, which irritates him greatly.

"Hey." He says, our standard greeting.

"Hey."

"You meeting your girl tonight?"

"Huh?"

"Ah, she's not your girl yet." He grins.

I stare back at him and he expands on his comment.

"You've been out more lately. Plus, you keep messing with your hair, guys only do that when they're in like with someone."

I continue staring at him, nonplussed by his freaky observation skills. I think, for the first time, about the downside of living with a psychology student, they know too much.

Isaac turns back to his cooking; he is nice enough to give me an easy pass if I don't want to talk about it. I watch him swear as he frantically starts chopping garlic, apparently having forgotten to add it before.

"I've been recommended that she maybe shouldn't be my girl." I say and leave it at that.

He doesn't say anything for a few moments but as he slips the garlic into a pan and starts stirring, he looks back at me through his mop of blonde. "By her?"

I shake my head.

"Maybe you should let her decide."

He makes it sound so simple, and maybe it should be but how am I supposed to ignore Ivy's advice. I remain silent and begin to stare at the pots on the hob, without really seeing them. Isaac gives me some slack again.

"I asked him out today."

"Yeah?"

"Yeah, we're going to go play pool."

I furrow my brow at him, "You suck at pool." I had discovered that very early on in knowing Isaac, last year. It's difficult to forget fearing for your life, from a cue ball that kept flying off the table in unpredictable directions.

Isaac grins. "I know; I was thinking he could teach me."

I grin back at him, trying hard not to say 'aw'. He hates that, but it is almost too cute. Instead I leave the room with a quick goodbye, making sure I don't crumble. I grab my coat on my way out, his words about letting her decide ringing in my head.

CHAPTER 14

I walk over to the house without listening to music. I go absolutely everywhere with earphones in and am getting slightly paranoid that I'll go deaf at twenty-five, plus I find the fact I never walk around musically unaided, means I appreciate all the little noises I would normally miss. I also find my breathing is lighter without music, I can hear the wind around me, so breathing it in feels more real, more present.

Their house is already about a thirty-minute walk from mine, but I still take the long route, going along a cycle path instead of cutting through streets. Normally when I walk anywhere, I'm in a rush, but today I don't even know what I'm heading to that house for, so it seems like the time to stroll the journey there, and reflect.

I am heading towards the house of people that could warp reality, or perception of reality, down to their appearances, and that I am just about fine with, but the concept of asking one of them out has me terrified. Figures. Finding out about superpowers, doable, normal teenage crap and I was done. I blame too much tv.

Whatever they are, they're good people. Cara, despite seeming to have very little regard for anyone, has never, at least to my knowledge, actually been unkind to someone. Ivy is a ball of fizzy sunshine. Lily is made of compassion. Sam seems to exude calm, despite his silent scarred, staring face. Ella appears terrified of the world but tries for other people and squeezes my hand. And Danny, okay, he isn't the nicest guy on the surface, but he had been the one to put that aside and drive me to the hospital when I needed to be there. If they are the people with the power, we could be doing a lot worse. Some politicians are definitely riskier choices and they're given countries.

In the end I decide to do what I'm doing with my walk and just take it slowly, notice what's happening and not rush anything. I don't have a problem with what me and Ella currently are, why stop that bit now, when it seems like what she's comfortable with too.

I arrive at the house, ready to just find out a bit about their history, like Ivy had suggested. I'd so far been mostly forgetting that I'd only gone to that house the second time to find out what they were. I need to focus on getting back to that.

The door remains closed for a long time after I knock on it, then it opens just enough to reveal Danny standing there, but not enough for me to walk passed him. He just looks at me, face passive and bored, one brow slightly raised in question as to what I am doing here.

"Is Ivy in?"

"No."

"Cara?"

"Nope."

"Anyone other than you?"

He shrugs his shoulders and positions his face into an annoying 'I don't know' style. I am at a loss for what to do, he doesn't seem to want me to come in, but then again, I don't particularly care about Danny's 'wants' too much.

I step inside.

Danny doesn't move, meaning I have to squeeze passed him awkwardly while he just looks at me. Which is impressively awkward. I half fall into the room when I get passed him and he finally moves to close the door.

The hall looks the same as it usually does, no piano, no leather sofas, just empty and big and white. Not knowing what to do once I'm inside, I start walking around the room, inspecting the walls as if there are artworks up and I'm in a gallery.

Danny doesn't make any noise, so I can't tell if he's moved or not, since I am avoiding looking in his direction, but the back of my neck has the tell-tale prickle of having someone stare at me. Eventually the feeling becomes too much, and I whirl back around to look at Danny, who is indeed staring at me, glaring at me, still standing by the door.

"What?" I ask, hoping for some reaction from him, some explanation as to why he acts weirdly with me, driving me to the hospital and acting a bit like a friend but in every other way acting with indifference edging towards cruelty. He managed to act relaxed around Ian but me, there is something in his way. He hasn't been cruel to me, but he seems just a nudge or a misplaced word away.

"What?" He replies, mimicking my tone.

I throw up my hands, suddenly very irritated. "What is your problem with me?!" My voice isn't raised that much above it's normal register, but it resonates around the entrance hall and the noise builds in anger with each bounce off the walls.

"You." He says, his voice as passive as his stupid face.

"What about me?" I'd asked and now I really want to know.

"Everything." Something about his tone then makes me feel that he is being honest, that giving any more detail is not necessary. His problem with me, is me, and everything I encompass.

My anger deflates, and I just stare at him, lost in how unfair that is. I'm struck by how strange it is to be hated, at least in part, for something you couldn't help, being you.

"Why?" My voice is strained by sadness, in agony to know the answer.

Danny just stares at first, looking into my face while he finds the words, finds an explanation for whole hearted disdain.

"I pity and envy you." The words don't bounce off the walls as much as the silence after them does.

"That doesn't make any sense."

"Hence the problem."

CHAPTER 15

The front door opens then, cracking the moment between us. Cara and Ivy stride into the room, arguing about something, causing them to take a while to notice Danny and I standing there, frozen, still looking at each other.

Their argument fizzles out into them simply looking between me and Danny, trying to fathom what is happening.

"What?" Asks Cara, dramatically throwing her hands into the air, not wanting to have to guess.

"Nothing." Says Danny, the finality unquestionable in his tone.

I remain quiet, stuck in the feeling his previous words had put me in. A feeling of being caught in between two separate feelings, so perfectly in between that I don't belong to either and drifting in limbo. Caught wondering what about he pities about me, and if that is the same, or different to what he envies.

Cara doesn't seem to notice my muteness however, and instead shrugs and starts filling us in on her day, unconcerned. "Well, anyway, I've just been shopping with Ivy, who was as helpless as usual, but I found some great stuff. Clothes are so up and down these days, but I have to admit I still prefer it to previous periods."

While Cara talks, I glance between her and Ivy, and notice something strange. "You don't have any bags?" I phrase it as a question, registering my surprise.

My words are met with even more confused look back.

"Duh." Says Cara, her words carrying enough sweetness,

it isn't quite rude, but I figure the sweetness is probably artificial.

Cara was wearing a blue sundress with a pattern of small sunflowers when she entered the house but is suddenly wearing pale pink corduroy trousers and a short sleeved white top, that reveals her smooth midriff, then in the next instant is wearing a button-down denim dress shaped in the style of a schoolgirl's pinafore dress. I quickly hold up my hand to halt her before she changes again, it hurts my eyes to adjust to every change.

"I get it." I say, blinking rapidly. "So, you don't actually buy anything, but you can make it seem like you're wearing it?" I continue, making sure I really get it.

"Yes." Says Ivy, sounding a little impressed I've understood so quickly.

I nod, taking another moment before saying to Ivy. "Is that similar to how you change your face? You put a different look on top?"

Ivy glances at Cara before she replies. "We'll cover that. Probably best to do it along with the history for it to make much sense."

I am surprised to have been denied an immediate answer, though it is just putting it off a little, I feel a pull in my stomach that the answer to this question might be the one to scare me. Make me scared of them.

It does remind me and reinforce the fact that I am going to be learning a probably quite important part about them today. So, I don't argue, not that I would've anyway.

"Okay." I say simply.

Ivy takes a few steps towards me and gestures to the door she wants me to head through, it's the one on the second right of the hall. The door next to the one I'd run through that first day. As I turn to follow her gesture, I notice that neither Cara or Danny move to come with us, and figure Ivy is my only teacher for the day.

It's a museum or, it looks exactly like a museum, covered in display cases as it is. It's a long hall, so long I can't quite make out the far end of it. The walls are painted forest green with dark wood panels running along them a third of the way up, the same dark wood covers the floor, and the high ceilings have subtle cornicing with elegant chandeliers placed down the hall, evenly sharing the light. Ivy stands next to me, by the doorway, allowing me a moment to take in my surroundings.

Once I have, I look down at her. We'd never really stood next to each other before, so I hadn't noticed how greatly our height differed, at six foot two I tower over her. In that moment it makes me feel oddly protective of her, though I know, even now, before I know anything, Ivy will never need my protection.

"So," She says, taking a big nervous breath in. "This is our history, as much as we've kept, which honestly isn't much but it's the best place to start."

I glance at the table closest to me, it holds a mixture of jewellery, bold and understated, and letters, scribbled and lengthy. Instead of asking about the table's contents, I decide to ask the question that seems to really be the place to begin. "When did your history start?"

"At the start." Says Ivy, green eyes peering into my own. "As best as we can tell, we started at the very start."

I am silent. Ivy takes my hand and very slowly inches me along the room.

"We weren't too aware of what was going on, we existed and that was pretty much it. Thought wasn't a thing for a long time, even time didn't factor for us for a while.

"Eventually we were here, on this beautiful rock and there was life. Life! Which was more than we started as. And somehow, we joined with it, we became alive, bodies and everything. We could move and see, and be, it felt a lot more like existing.

"Then humans came along, and you changed the game. You were terrifying but fascinating. So, we tried you on, we looked like you and then evolved with you. We stayed for everything you built, watched you form language and a whole new culture, and we were so wrapped up in awe of you we never left. We're still here, still human, with you."

Ivy's voice had grown with enthusiasm as she spoke, and she'd let go of me, moving around, gesticulating wildly, but as she stopped speaking all the excitement left her.

I've gone pale, I know I have, it's one of the few things I know as my brain breaks down trying to accept her words. Trying to accept how far from human they all truly are, how they'd apparently just become like us, on a whim, after being whatever they were before, just existing, not even alive. My mind, bizarrely, comes up with the image of the stereotypical alien form, climbing into a human suit. It is a disgusting image in the sudden realness of it, even though I am aware that wasn't what they had done, but it is the closest image my brain could work with.

Ivy steps towards me, face full of concern, and I try to let her, but I take a step back, right into the table of jewellery and letters, causing an oddly loud jangling noise. I turned to the noise, for something to do, anything. Wincing at the fact I can't look at her.

"Don't be scared of us." Whispers Ivy, I can almost hear tears in her voice.

I don't look back at her, I can't. Fear isn't the word, I don't fear them at all, it is just too much, they are too much to simply accept. They're so far away from me, even with Ivy standing less than a foot behind, I feel like space is expanding between us, between me and my friend.

While I continue not looking at her, Ivy talks anyway, trying to push herself back to me. "We feel so at home here. Being human let us find each other. And living like you, it

lets us live in a way which is so much more than just surviv-
ing and being, there's belonging here."

Ivy pauses again and staring into the sparkling stone of
what looks like an engagement ring I force out, "You don't
have to justify yourself to me." I mean the words, of course
I do, they can live however they want, and they are good,
fundamentally they are all good. I have no right or desire to
argue against the faces, the species, they choose to wear. At
this moment I am even struggling to distinguish why I can't
look at Ivy, but as I relent and look into her face it comes to
me.

"But you're not just like us, Lily said we called you Gods.
You're more than us, and I want to know what that means."

Ivy shuts her eyes, but I can still see how close she is
to crying when they shut. "There were times when we let
people see what we could do. They wished for better lives
and sometimes we could help, we could make the sun feel
less blinding, make the little food they had seem to go further, we made things feel a bit easier, and it helped people
survive. Belief helps people to fight.

"People crowned us Gods for that, and it built into something so big, they expected salvation." Ivy's voice trails off,
regret and bitterness forcing their way in before she can stop.

"Which you couldn't give?"

"No."

"You could only give pretence, little things to make it
seem like you were helping."

"We were helping!"

"You couldn't save them!"

"Nothing could!"

"But you can change things! Effect things. That day, Cara,
she stopped time or something in my lecture theatre, everyone froze."

Ivy grimaces against my words before answering them.

"That's a scare tactic. A trick. Instead of effecting your perception she stops everyone else perceiving things for a second, halts their brains, it pauses them, makes it look like we freeze them. It's nothing."

I try and reconcile that thought, it had been the thing that made me believe in them, believe they could do something. I stop then, unable to fight her anymore, I sway where I stand. My next words coming out as a whisper.

"You can't save her."

The anger and most of the frustration leave Ivy's face, her face instead becomes a question mark, asking the obvious question of 'who?'

I think about Katie, beautiful Katie who is the best six-year-old ever and isn't going to get to turn seven. She takes over my mind, and the last, small part of me that believed, believed something would come along and save her, just because it should, dies. Not even the 'Gods' could save her. My body slumps against the table behind me, my limbs trembling, but I ignore them and the noise the table makes this time. My ears are filling with white noise.

Ivy tentatively reaches out and touches my arm, when I don't resist her touch, she moves to fully encapsulate me in a hug. Slowly I raise my arms and hold her too, then the tears come. They gush out of me.

The two of us stand there for a long moment, Ivy holding me together, while my body and brain do everything they can to crumble. When the peak wave has crashed over me, I release Ivy and stand on my own again. That's when I notice the door behind us is open and Danny is standing there, staring again.

"What?" I say, refusing to put an apology in my voice for the mess I am, and also realising how much that word has been repeated today.

Danny doesn't speak but looks at Ivy, apparently signalling something, as she proceeds to leave the room, giving my arm a final squeeze before she does. The door closes, and it is just me and him.

"She's why." Says Danny, his voice quiet and nervous. I didn't know he was capable of sounding nervous.

"Ivy?" I say, confused.

"Katie."

I say nothing.

"The pain you feel because of her, I'm so sorry for that, but the rest of it, living like you do, I can't stand it, watching you, anyone, have it."

"You live."

"Not like you, not beginning to end. We've just got the middle."

"So, you have a problem with everyone?"

"Yes."

I don't reply, I don't want to. I'm still too busy struggling with my loss of hope, I don't need to be told I'm envied for it right now. Instead I walk out, he lets me, and I walk right out the building. Not bothering with any social convention, saying goodbye, being relatively polite, I just leave and head to where I need to be, to Katie.

CHAPTER 16

Katie is thrilled to see me, so is my mum but she is also confused. I'd gotten the bus right to my house, not thinking about the fact it was late on Monday and I had class the next day, plus had been here just yesterday. When I walked in the house, they were all sitting at the dining table in our kitchen eating dinner, a dinner which basically looked like a chicken salad, very healthy and not at all tasty. Katie jumps down from her seat immediately and grabs my knees in a hug, I return it and give a small smile to my parents, my way of hello.

Without a word my mum gets up and gets a plate for me, piling on some of the chicken salad from the kitchen counter that holds the extra supply, she doesn't hand it to me but places it on the table and returns to her own seat. I wrestle Katie off of me and scoop her back into her seat, taking my own next to her.

"How are classes going?" Asks my dad, who's just continued eating since my arrival, and is still focussing on his fork when he speaks to me.

"Good, didn't have that much on today." I reply, trying to act as normally as I can, that's part of the reason I've come home, for the normalcy.

My dad nods, and my mum takes over, "What about tomorrow? I thought Tuesday was a busy day for you."

It is, relatively, I have three classes during the day quite early on, then I normally go along to play a casual game of football with a few friends, so we can pretend we were active people. I'd missed it last week because I'd gone, there. I can't think about that. "It is." I say, staring at my plate, beginning to pick at the greenery in front of me, with my fork.

My mum doesn't say any more, but I can practically feel her antenna go up, worrying about me. I make a mental note to put her off that at a later point in the night.

Unaware that anything even remotely unusual is going on, Katie takes over the conversation. She always does that at meal times, she thinks it distracts us from the fact that she isn't eating anything on her plate. Katie doesn't have an appetite anymore, but she always pretends she does. Even yesterday when she'd covered her plate of pancakes with sugar, I'd known that even if my mum hadn't swooped in to make Katie's plate heathier, she wouldn't have eaten any of it, she wouldn't have been able to take the smell of all that sugar, but she still enjoyed making up the plate.

Anyway, she starts informing us about the fairy she'd spotted in our garden earlier in the day, filling us in on every detail about it, it's pretty dress and sparkly wings, and all about fairy culture. I smile through the whole story, enjoying how sure of herself she seems, she would've made a great writer or maybe a lawyer, with an imagination like that, after that thought, my smile becomes sadder but still true, I love just watching Katie ramble. My dad switches off a little, he is a good dad, but he is a bit too much of a realist to listen to talk about fairies. My mum tries to smile through it, but I can see in her eyes that she's already been told this story at least twice already today and is running low on enthusiasm.

"Do you know any fairies?" Is how Katie finishes her story, looking around at us all, honestly curious.

My parents don't say anything, I see them glance between each other in the corner of my eye, so I pipe in. "No, meeting fairies is really rare you're lucky. I have met a pixie though, they're great and just as much fun."

"Will." My dad says warningly, trying to cut me off from filling Katie's head with nonsense. I understand why, I really do, believing in magic was good for little kids but they would normally grow out of it with time, Katie doesn't have time. My dad takes this to mean Katie should know the truth about the world while she can, but I disagree.

I know the truth now, more than he does, I'd learned it earlier today, and had the belief stripped of me and it feels like an open wound, burning me. If Katie can believe, even wrongly, in anything, I am totally up for that.

So, I ignore my dad's warning tone and focus only on Katie's now awed face. "See, fairies are really small so they're easy to miss, but pixies they're just a little smaller than us, still bigger than you though, so they can blend in, but they don't like to. The one I know, she's made of sugar, all sweetness and fizz. She's got violet spiky hair and so much energy, she runs around making people happy all day, that's her job." It hurts a little to talk about Ivy like this when I know I'd yelled at her earlier, but I feel like with the hug, we'd forgiven each other. Even though I'm unsure how I feel about them overall just now, I'm relieved by that.

Katie is still looking at me with awe, her mind racing with the idea of pixies. "Is Agnes a pixie?" She asks, in a secretive whisper. Agnes is Katie's paediatric nurse most of the time she's in the hospital, she is short, round and warm and always made me think of freshly made cookies when I see her.

I smile and lean into Katie, also making my voice a secretive whisper. "You know; I think she might be."

My dad slams down his fork, not violently but enough to make us all turn to him. I see that my window of openly indulging the idea of magic is shut for the night, at least in front of him. We return to talking about normal topics, I try explaining my philosophy class to everyone but just make everyone confused, including myself, and my mum talks us through, in excruciating detail, how she made tonight's meal.

My mum used to work, she had a good job in a bank, giving people advice on what investment was best for them and how best to balance money, it was a small local bank as well, not a big faceless one. She'd worked there since before I was born and loved it, feeling like she was helping, but when Katie was diagnosed, she quit the next day, knowing in her bones that she had to put everything into helping her. My dad probably would've left his job if my mum hadn't, he's the manager of an office, I'm never sure what the office does, anyway he hates it, but our family needed his income more than our mum's, so he stayed. Family friends always talk about how much my mum sacrificed for Katie in leaving a job she loved, and she did, but I think my dad doesn't get enough credit for staying at work, not even looking for a job that fits him better, he sacrifices his life nine to five, so we are taken care of twenty-four seven.

After we finish eating, and Katie manages to clear half her plate, I stay in the kitchen with my mum to do the dishes, while my dad takes Katie through to the living room to watch tv while making funny commentary to each other, which is more my dad's style of fun.

I've just filled the sink when my mum starts on me, I'd forgotten about her worry earlier. "Will, is everything okay?"

I swallow the urge to sigh heavily, and to totally lie. "Yeah, it's just a weird time at the moment, you know?" I add the 'you know' so it seems like there is even the slightest possibility that she can.

My mum reaches up and holds my cheek for a second, she isn't a small woman but always appears so next to me, and looks right at me, searching my eyes with her matching green ones for anything more. She doesn't find it. "We're here for you, Will. I know we're busy with Katie so don't always stay too on top of your life but we're still here."

I nod slowly, "Thanks, Mum."

We continue with the dishes in silence, just sharing the moment together, a moment which is made even sweeter by the sounds of my dad and Katie bursting into laughter the next room over.

There isn't much on tv, so I take Katie upstairs just half an hour later, to get ready for bed while my parents settle in for watching the news together. I brush my teeth while Katie does, mostly to make sure she does it for long enough and then search for a book to read her, while she gets changed into her pyjamas, I don't feel like I have it in me to make up a story tonight, not without accidentally making it sad, and Katie doesn't need that.

When Katie's head pops out from her pyjama top, she stops short staring out the window. "Cat!"

I whip around to look out the window too, there is indeed a cat sitting on her window sill, which is one floor up. While I wonder how on earth a cat managed to get up there, I move to usher Katie out of the room. "Why don't you go give Mum and Dad a final hug goodnight, while I sort this?"

Katie visibly wants to stay with the cat, but she realises, after catching my eye that I am not going to budge. For all I know the cat is violent, I am dealing with it alone. Once Katie begrudgingly heads downstairs, I walk over to the window for a proper look at the cat. It doesn't look feral, it's a tabby with jade green eyes, very familiar jade green eyes, and it is staring straight at me with a tilted head.

I crouch down so I am eye level with the cat. "You can't be serious." I mutter. The cat nods its little head at me, I jump back, then rub my eyes tiredly, sighing.

Unable to believe what I am doing, I reach out and open the window, letting a cat into my sister's room. Before I can think better of it and shut the window again, the cat flops down onto the floor, almost elegantly but it doesn't quite stick the landing, like any normal cat would. As I turn around to get a look at it on the floor, it suddenly isn't there anymore, or anywhere.

Ivy, back in her pixie look from when we met, stands very close to me, looking at me with those jade green eyes. I take a stumbling step back and fight the urge to swear in shock, though it isn't a total shock, worried Katie might hear me. "What are you doing here?"

"Checking up on you."

"As a cat?!"

"Makes staring in your windows less creepy."

I want to argue back, but I end up laughing instead, it really is difficult to feel negatively around Ivy, apart from when she explains some impossible to grasp truths and makes hope disappear, but then again it is probably better to learn it from her than Danny or even Cara.

Ivy looks around the room, like she has to see it to realise something, and then she looks back at me. "I hadn't put it together, about Katie. Danny didn't tell us and neither did Ian. We didn't know why you had to go to hospital that day, how serious things were for you." She says it like an apology and I guess it is. Explaining what they are, in a way was just explaining who they are to me, she hadn't realised I was searching for more.

I smile back at her, sadly. "I probably should've made it clearer, why I wanted to know more about you. I liked thinking maybe there was something you could do, or if there was someone I could blame for everything. But I'm not good at telling other people." It's true, I hadn't even told Ian or anyone else from school or university officially, some had just been around my family enough to pick up on it.

"So, are we okay?" Ivy asks, tentatively.

I consider it. "Yeah, I think so. Maybe more so, now that I know you can't help." I didn't mean the words to be hurtful but from Ivy's reaction, my words stung her.

"We can help, just not in the way you wanted."

"I didn't... "

"I know." Ivy says, smiling a little, showing she isn't too hurt.

The door begins to open then, and immediately there is a cat in the room with me instead of Ivy. I can't quite bring myself to think of the cat as Ivy, though I guess that it is. Katie ducks her head into the room checking she is allowed in, but upon seeing the cat, she abandons care for what she is allowed to do and runs over to it. I don't know how the cat will take to being cuddled by my six-year-old sister, but I hear a distinct purr come from it a second later.

"Can we keep her?" Asks Katie, face full of shining hope. I see the cat's eyes widen and laugh.

"No, I'm sure she's got a home to go to." I say, trying to treat this scenario like it is just a cat we are discussing.

Katie pouts but I gently take the cat off of her and tell her to get into bed. She tries arguing that I haven't read her a story yet, but I tell her the cat excitement has surely been better and she doesn't have a comeback. Plus, I figure it is probably best to get the cat/Ivy out the house as soon as I can, before my mum sees her and freaks.

I awkwardly close the door behind me with the cat in my arms, which makes me realise the peculiarity of the fact I am essentially carrying Ivy around my house, I quickly try to push that thought out of my head, at least until I can put her down.

Pausing on the landing, I listen out for my parents in the living room and hear them arguing about which weatherman they prefer, I roll my eyes at their conversation but am glad they are distracted. I move slowly down the stairs, trying to avoid making too much noise and deciding that I will never become so boring that I find weathermen arguments stimulating. When I reach the bottom of the stairs, I dart quickly to the back door, deciding opening that will be much easier to explain to my parents if they hear.

I drop the cat to the ground as soon as I get the door open, and again she doesn't quite stick the landing, I felt a twinge of guilt at treating her too much like a cat. "Sorry."

Once again, the cat turns into Ivy and is in front of me, shaking herself out, her in the garden, me still in the house. "It's okay."

The next moment passes awkwardly, as we both try to find a way to say goodbye that doesn't risk being an acceptable final one.

"So, see you tomorrow?" Ivy tries.

"Probably not tomorrow, hectic day." I reply, hating to say no. "The day after or something?" I wish I hadn't added the last bit, that makes it seem like I might just be saying it as a blow off.

Ivy begins turning to go, probably just to get away from the awkward, but she looks back after one step. "You know, what I said today, that was part of why I said you probably shouldn't ask out Ella."

The words surprise me, I'd completely forgotten about Ella, well not forgotten, but a lot of other things had taken up the forefront of my mind. "There's a lot more than just that to you guys isn't there?" I ask, sounding apprehensive.

Ivy nods, and I take a deep breath in. "Think I can take it?" I ask, my voice a bit more light-hearted this time, smothering the worry I feel.

Ivy smiles. "You might be one of the few who can." With that, she turns away from me, properly this time, and walks over to the back wall of my garden before hopping over it easily and vanishing. I stand looking out at the wall for a second more before smiling and shutting the door.

As I walk up to my own room and get myself slowly ready for bed, I think back to Katie's smiling face when she hugged the cat and decide that Ivy is right, even if just a bit, she is capable of helping, in the same way I am, helping keep a little joy and faith in a little girl's world.

I settle into bed and decide I'm not done getting to know the people that live in that Victorian house, and that maybe I am being too quick to judge. They might be able to save Katie, in one way or another.

CHAPTER 17

When I walk into class on Tuesday, I expect to see Ian waving at me, he is frighteningly punctual and always gets a seat before me, but instead I see Cara waving at me from the seat next to him. Surprised, I head over to them and take my seat, smiling a general hello at my friends, before turning just to Cara.

"Since when do you sit here?" I ask, keeping the accusation out my voice.

Cara smiles back at me. "Since now. You earned it." She says it with her usual flirty teasing.

I settle into my seat happily but as the lecturer starts up, I have a worrying realisation and nudge Cara gently with my elbow. "You know that English assignment we were meant to do?"

Cara doesn't turn to me, but her eyes widen in matching realisation. We've been so caught up in meeting to allow me to get know them that we've totally forgotten and ignored the initial academic purpose of me going to her house. A project, which is due tomorrow.

The rest of the lecture is spent with a heavy silence between us, with me taking half-hearted notes while I stress about getting our project done. I am very sure that the other people in our group have still done less than us, so there is no point checking in with them.

Our lecturer rounds up, finally, and we are free to go. Cara immediately grabs my arm, looking as frazzled as she is capable, meaning a single strand of hair has come loose of her ponytail, and it looks awfully red compared to normal. "Okay, we need to do some serious work today."

Ian has stood up next to us and looks over, confused, as he puts his bag over his shoulder. "Haven't you guys been doing that like every day for a week?"

I look up at him unsure how to explain that that hasn't been what's going on, without risking him assuming the very wrong thing. Cara doesn't have the same problem, "We kept getting distracted."

Ian's eyebrows rise but he doesn't say any more. I try to see if there is any jealousy in his eyes, I know he liked Cara before, but then I remember his lingering arm around Ivy the day before which re-establishes my desire to talk to him.

As we all leave the lecture theatre in a clump of people, I explain to Cara that I have a busy morning of classes, and the football game. I expect her to brush off the mention of the game and say I am free then but instead she says she'll come along and start work on it there. Part of me feels a little weird about the idea of her sitting on the side lines for me, that's something that only girlfriends do, if any of us have them, but I push the feeling down, knowing Cara is aware that isn't the case with us.

People split off towards their different classes, or just to go home, and I stay with Ian, glad for an early chance to ask about Ivy. I decided to forget about tact. "So, Ivy?"

Ian is silent for a moment and just barely nods his head, then he turns his head to me. "That okay?"

I nod back, surprised by how unspoken this conversation is going. Ian is normally the kind of guy to talk big about everything and go over every detail of stuff, to see him say essentially nothing when I ask about a girl is strange. We keep walking in silence for a while, and I try to think why Ian is being so quiet, then I remember when he'd had to drag details about Ella from me and that I haven't given him any

110

real details since, and I feel bad. I don't want me and Ian to have anything we don't talk about.

"I think I've decided to play it cool with Ella." I say, testing the waters.

"You're not cool." Says Ian, smiling slightly.

"Yeah but I don't want her to know that."

Ian laughs at that. "I think I'm going to play it cool with Ivy."

"She's cool."

"I know! It's intimidating."

I laugh, and nudge Ian jovially in the arm, similar to the way Ivy always does with me. Then I think back to the day before. "She's complicated, you know?"

"Some girls are worth complicated."

Ella's face flashes behind my eyes and I don't argue. We settle into an easy silence, the only noise between us being the sound of our feet on the paved walkway across campus.

I think about Ian and Ivy together, and it makes a nice picture. I imagine them playing air hockey together getting competitive or talking animatedly over a drink at a bar, it looks like it works in my head, I hope it would in real life. My train of thought doesn't stop there, I begin to wonder what Ivy and the others do with relationships, long term ones, they don't need to age, and they change around so much with their lives, could they ever have that kind of life with someone. The thought causes a pit in my stomach to open, one I can't quite place the exact reason for, but I feel that it relates to Danny.

By the time we sit down for our history lecture, things feel back to normal with Ian and me, I allow myself a little sigh of relief.

I find that with the introduction of Cara, Ivy and the others to my life, the rest of it has come to feel so mundane. Everything in between seeing them and seeing Katie, feels just like something to get through rather than a part of my life, probably a distinction that shouldn't be there, especially when it comes to university, but I have no idea how to change it.

The rest of my classes pass without too much brain power, even philosophy, recent days and revelations have burst my mind and my reality so wide open I just take in everything the lecturer throws at me. I grab a quick sandwich with Ian and Jack from the campus shop and we head over to the football fields that sit behind the accommodation building.

I missed football the previous week for working with Cara, and I've honestly been feeling the loss of it. I feel the need to turn my mind off for a bit and just kick something.

The group of us that play aren't very good, the games usually end with an argument over whether or not a goal counts, rather than lasting any substantial amount of time, but it's good fun. Every week this guy, Simon, who is annoying as anything, but well organised, divides us up into teams using a different rule, normally something about our shirts or shoes that makes up equal teams. It means we change around a lot, and there is no chance of leaving anyone out. It's a good system but I'm always a little unnerved when Simon stares us down to find a rule

He looks around at us all, face scrunched up trying to find something to suit, after a moment he un-scrunches his face and rolls his eyes. "Everyone stick up your hands."

We all look around at each other confused, then follow his orders, all in either a half-hearted or awkward manner. He keeps his eagle eyes on us, then points at a few not including me. "You guys were first, you're a team." Then he uses his hand to usher them towards their apparent side of the pitch.

Those of us remaining gather in a make shift huddle on our side for a rough game plan. As Ian throws his arm around me to drag my tall self, down to the other's heights, I notice

Cara has appeared by the edge of the pitch and sat herself elegantly on a small bench, scattered papers all around her.

Game commences and we all run around wildly. Jack was put on the other team to us and I am playing off him, which means we immediately became five-year olds and just chase each other. Ten minutes into play, Ian scores a goal for our team and we all jump on him in celebration, which leads to a mess of us on the grass.

When we resume play, Ian is covered in grass stains, and I notice that Cara is standing and seems to be following the game. As the ball passes up and down the pitch, Cara begins to cheer for my team, attempting to egg us on, she does it like an American cheerleader and I notice the other guys on my team start to put a lot more effort into their game.

The match ends when Simon takes down a guy on the other team, who lays on the floor clutching his knee. Cara had encouraged him a bit too much. A few people stay with the guy and the rest of us disperse to hunt down drinks of water. I walk over to my bag which is near Cara and give her an exhausted smile as I start rifling in it for my bottle.

"Didn't expect you to be a big football fan." I say, once I've partially quenched my thirst.

"Sexist." Replies Cara smiling sweetly. "I've always loved the game, there's always something so childish about it."

I cut her a look. "Yeah, until the guys start caring too much about the pretty girl watching."

Cara's smile turns to a mischievous smirk. "That's part of the fun too."

I grin back at her, and shake my head saying, "You really are a dangerous woman."

"Ah so you've cottoned on?"

I don't reply and just shake my head as I take another long swig of my water.

Jack and Ian come over to me, too tired to attempt any kind of sneak attack from behind. They offer tired waves to Cara, obviously not having enough energy to try for a conversation. We really are nerdier than I usually let myself believe, we barely played for half an hour.

"So how hard is the project looking?" I ask, looking at the many papers lying on the bench, apprehensively.

"I think we'll be fine." Says Cara, completely unconcerned. My antenna goes up but I decide not to argue with her.

CHAPTER 18

Jack and Ian want time to cool down before they head home, so ask about walking with us to Cara's. She happily agrees so I do too, and try not to think about them seeing the inside of the house.

We all walk very slowly, enjoying the faint breeze the day offers, as we do I realise, that despite the fact it seems that Cara is beginning to hang out with us, the same as Ivy is, it is very different. Ivy is so easy to be around, she just fits in with the rest of us, Cara holds such a performance in everything she does, she always seems like the main attraction to our side act, it's still fun but not as easy.

Cara has decided to have a little fun with Jack so is walking backwards, in front of us, facing him as he speaks about the game, with her hands behind her back and her face showing far greater interest than I'm sure she feels. Poor Jack is getting flustered as he speaks and tripping up on his words. Ian is stifling a laugh next to me, at Jack's reaction to the attention, and I am attempting not to do the same because Ian would have acted exactly the same a few days ago.

As we take a shortcut through a park I begin to wonder where Cara's flirtiness comes from, an image of her living as the goddess of love as she passed through all human cultures runs through my mind. I continue laughing to myself silently, and internally decide to give Jack a break, he may be dealing with the actual Aphrodite here.

Halfway through a new story of Jack's, Cara suddenly

changes tactics and cuts him off to speak to me. "Will, what level of cheating are you comfortable with?" She asks.

I blink back at her for a moment, before coming out with. "Not very high."

Cara rolls her eyes at me, disappointed, but not surprised. "It's just asking Sam for some help, he loved the time period our project's on, he was so into the arts scene then."

I am surprised by Cara's phrasing, our project is on the literature of the Romantics, meaning it was stuff written in and around the 1800s, not something she should be talking about as though she, or well Sam, could have been there. However, Ian and Jack don't notice anything, Jack has composed himself quickly and switched to telling his story to Ian as soon as Cara cut him off, and they apparently didn't hear her. Cara winks at me.

"I guess we can ask Sam but he can't write it for us or anything." I say, trying to act casual, a small part of my brain wondering how Sam, who doesn't speak, would be able to offer us his help.

Cara just winks again, slightly infuriatingly, and then inserts herself back into what Jack and Ian are talking about, done with me after her bit of fun. Interacting with Cara always feels more like a game than a conversation, and it's a game I am pretty slow to play.

When we get close to Cara's house, she stops talking to the guys again and instead flips out a phone, which I hadn't realised she owned and starts flicking through it distractedly. Ian and Jack take this as a hint, surprising me, since they are usually not the type to leave the side of a pretty girl without a fight, making me wonder how cool Ian finds Ivy.

Once they leave our side with waves of goodbye, accidentally highlighting the sweat stains under their arms, Cara's phone vanishes again. "Did you get rid of them deliberately?" I ask, shuffling my bag nervously over my own under arms and pointedly looking at where her phone had been. "And since when do you have a phone?"

Cara grins, her brazen eyes flickering to my nervous movements, making me curse them. "Yes, I thought you might start hyperventilating if they got too close to the house. And I have a phone when I need one."

"If it's not a real phone then how can anyone get in touch with you when they need to?" I ask, me having to show up to their residence whenever I wanted to talk to them was honestly irksome, though the idea of messaging them also seems bizarre.

Cara pouts at me, making me notice, not how pretty it made her face looked, but it's lack of effect on me. In the end she just shrugs. "It's never been an issue until now."

I'm working up to ask how often they make friends with humans and wondering if subtly referring to them not as human would offend her, when we reach the house. Walking through the door I expect the same vaulted ceilinged room I've grown accustomed too, but instead I screech to a halt in the doorway of what looks like a cottage. A cosy, bare wood room with mismatched furniture and a roaring fireplace has met us instead. On the sofa Lily and Sam are sat, cuddled together staring absently into the flames ahead.

Once I get used to the new surroundings, I immediately start finding anywhere to look, that isn't the couple in front of me, they aren't doing anything but it still seems like a moment my gaze shouldn't intrude upon. Cara does not have this issue, and claps her hands together, loudly.

"Sam the man." Her voice rocks the tiny room and causes Lily and Sam to fall right out of their sofa in surprise. I try to muffle my snort, I hadn't thought either of them could demonstrate such a lack of elegance.

They both regain their footing with more class, and as I watch them the room changes in a blink back to the usual entrance way. My eyes burn in the sudden brightness and I wish it would go back to being cosy rather than grand. Cosy in a house always feels more realistic to me. Realistic helps with these people, but I guess so does the fact their abilities are normalising to me.

"Sorry," Says Lily, brushing non-existent creases off the skirt of her sun dress. "We know the hall isn't meant to change that much, we just didn't want to move."

I cut them all a look of confusion, surprised there are apparently rules to their home. Cara explains. "Interior decoration is a nightmare to agree on, so we don't change the common areas."

I have a sudden memory of an argument between Eric, Isaac and me about wall decoration in our living room/kitchen when we first moved into our flat. I guess all flatmates must argue about that kind of thing. I nod and Cara returns her attention to Sam. "Any chance you can help us with our English assignment? Romantics, you loved them."

Sam gives Cara a kindly smile, recognising the slight plea in her voice, from his expression I highly doubt that is the first time Cara has asked for help on homework. He holds out his hand, and as Cara focuses her eyes on it, several books layer over his outstretched palm and Sam has to bring up his other hand to take the weight. Glancing at the spines I can see I notice a number of books from our reading list for the class, I also realise I've only read two of the many there. I really need to be spending more time on university. Sam rifles through the books, tossing some over his shoulder, they vanish before hitting the floor, when he is down to three books he stares at them for a long moment, leafing briefly through the pages as though reminding himself, then hands them back to Cara, all without a word. Like always, the silence around Sam isn't harsh or negative, just strong and present. For only the second time in looking at Sam I allow myself to properly look at the scar that governs so much of his face, it seems like a part of his silence, possibly the reason for it, and I wonder why, when they can choose their whole appearance he has chosen to create or keep that act of violence upon his features.

Instead of asking about it, I turn my face away, the act making me feel like a coward, and turn to watch Cara inspect the books Sam has given back to her, relieved to see they include the two I have actually read. As Cara handles the books she takes out a folded piece of paper, covered in minute writing. I lean over to inspect it and realise it has notes on the books she holds, Sam's notes I assume.

Looking up, Cara beams. "Thank you." I turned to Sam as well and smile at him.

"You really liked those books." It sounds stupid as I say it, but his writing is so small on the paper, he's shoved so much information onto it that the paper is practically black. Having so much to say seems to mean a lot from Sam, or maybe he writes all the time and I just don't know it.

Sam just smiles back and nods. The warmth of him, makes me wonder even more about the scar on his cheek as it stretches with his mouth. I really don't feel like I have the right to know but that doesn't mean I don't have the right to ask. Cara is still looking over the notes, like they are the map to buried treasure, the treasure of an easy A, and Lily has moved over to read them as well, smiling in appreciation of Sam's knowledge.

I raise my hand slowly, up to my own cheek, attempting to make the gesture a whisper like my next words. "Can I ask?"

Sam's smile doesn't shrink and the warmth remains but a tension rises in his face. Stepping back from the girls he permits me to follow him to one of the doorways on the right hand side of the entrance. I wonder if the rooms beyond those doors stay fixed or if the doors themselves just act as access points, I also notice that Cara and Lily don't follow us though they have both looked up. My stomach twists as the door Sam has reached opens.

CHAPTER 19

It isn't a room exactly. As I step through the doorway, I simply enter space, white pure space, floor extending only so far as Sam and I require it. While I look around and search for something in the nothing, it stops being nothing.

Suddenly I am in a field, up to my waist in cotton. In the rush of it appearing around me, a plant appears in the place of my hand, it nicks at my finger and I pull it away sharply, spotting a few drops of blood blossoming on the white of the cotton as well as along a fresh cut on my fingers, running along next to the nail. I am about to bring my finger to my mouth when a loud noise distracts me from my pain.

A harsh voice had shouted out, and raising my head I see a tall broad man screaming in the face of a child, only a few metres ahead of me. The child too holds a slightly bloodied hand and tears shine down his dark round cheeks, his hand is held to his chest but I can see beneath him, a basket of picked cotton with dots of red across it. The man continues shouting as he moves ever closer to the boy, his voice so filled with anger and a southern accent I can't make out the words. I try to move towards them both but find my feet stuck to the ground like they had been outside the party when I'd been stopped from rushing to Katie. The crying boy looks around her age.

As I watch, stuck and frozen by my horror, I see the man lift a hand to the child, a hand that is not empty. Realisation burns white across my mind and I start to fight against my feet, trying to lunge forward and stop what is going to happen. What had already happened. As the top half of my body falls forward in my effort, the cotton plants in front of me cut at my face and cover my vision as the sound of a whip slices the air.

A scream is torn from my body as again the space around me turns to clear white. I am on my knees, breathing hard, hearing the violence of that sound rattle through my head, which I try to raise to Sam, Sam and his scarred dark round cheek. "That was you?" I croak out, pleading to be wrong.

Sam shakes his head looking down at me. A figure appears a distance away from us, one I recognise vaguely as being part of the background in the scene I just witnessed. A man on horseback, looking over as he passed through the scene. I sit up from my position and look at the expression on the figure's face, mild interest and disdain. I turn back to Sam and can't match the two faces I see as possibly being from the same entity, but as I continue to stare into his face, I know the one he is wearing does belong to that child I had just seen hurt, and I also recognise the expression behind Sam's eyes. Regret.

"You wear his face as penance?" I ask, trying not to sound disgusted though the idea does turn my stomach.

"He wears it to remember." The voice comes from behind me, and I turn in my seated position to see that Cara and Lily have joined us. Cara was the one to speak.

The image of the crying child flashes across my mind's eye, so vividly I have to shut my eyes, how could something like that ever be forgotten? But from the back of my mind comes the memory that these beings before me are immortal, they have lived through history and endured each day of it, not everything could be remembered. Another image drifts into my mind's eye of the room Ivy had briefly shown me, of the objects they had saved, and I wonder how much that was necessary for sentimentality and how much it was for simply remembering and keeping track of the lives they had all lived.

Wanting to stand up again I hold out my hand to Sam and he pulls me up, as he does, I clap my other hand on his arm and look him in the eye. "You're a good man." I can't possibly know how true those words really are, but you can never be truly sure with anyone. The regret in his eyes for being a bystander of horrible history still shines in his eyes, and in every other moment of looking at him I have seen nothing but warmth and kindness, even if, in some small way, that kindness comes from atonement, it comes from somewhere good.

Sam's grip on my hand tightens before he releases me and I know that my words mean something to him, which is enough.

"Aw bromance." Says Cara, in sing song mockery. Her voice ruins the moment but it also breaks the tension. We all smile and leave the room together, making our way back.

CHAPTER 20

It takes a shockingly short amount of time for me and Cara to finish our assignment. We sit at a desk that appears in the entrance way and read over Sam's notes and voice our own opinions, we also discuss the layout we'd use to put together all our points. Just as I am about to suggest we get a computer to start writing up the proper thing, Cara does a fancy flourish with her hand, always one for dramatics, and hands me a few pieces of paper, which contains a fully typed up assignment, combining all our points perfectly. I hold it in my hand looking awed and Cara collapses in her seat laughing at my face.

Her head lays for a moment on the table and as she lifts it, she has to move her hair back off her face. It is such an honest moment from Cara, who normally maintains her aura of womanly perfection, even when it's just me and her, and not in any way required. It's the first moment I figure she might consider me a friend, in the way I consider her, and I place the pieces of paper down on the desk, smiling to myself.

With the assignment finished I assume I'll head back to my flat and attempt to work on some of the other assignments and class reading that have been piling up since my first time in this house. As I begin to reach to get my jacket off the back of my chair, Danny appears jogging down the stairs towards us.

"Pool?" He asks, eyes only on Cara, who nods. She bounces up from her seat, which instantly vanishes alongside the desk, I quickly stand up, expecting my chair to vanish too. Which it does, but probably only because I have stood.

Sam and Lily re-enter the room from a different doorway than they left through earlier, again making me wonder about the make-up off the house's layout. Ivy buzzes in after them, playfully swatting them both on the back as she races around ahead of them. Before she disappears through another doorway I hear her excitedly shout, "Pool!"

We all laugh and I again make to put my jacket on, having taking it with me when exiting my seat. Everyone else begins to move towards the door Ivy had vanished through and I aim for the exit, readying myself to wave them good bye. Instead I find Danny's hand around my arm and him steering me towards the other door.

Startled I am pushed into the pool room from my first, and only, solitary endeavour into the house. The others smile at my entrance. "So, you like me now?" I aim at Danny, unsure whether the teasing in my voice is necessary. He glares in return so I think it is.

"He's just accepted that we like you." Answers Ivy, a teasing matching my own in her voice. I grin at her and pick up a cue from the stand next to the door.

The room is lined with multiple pool tables but we only use two. Having four people playing and two hovering, waiting to go next, with an agreed-winners stay on rule unless someone is too good. I am only average at pool so suspect I'll just get a couple games of play time, they are bound to have had a lot more time to practice, and for all I know, had invented the game.

I'm just leaning on my cue watching Ivy set up for our game, with her tongue slightly sticking out, when Ella walks into the room, I almost drop the stick and Ivy snorts. Ella just smiles around at all of us and takes a seat in a stuffed leather arm chair resting against the wall between the two tables, tucking her legs under her as she does so.

After waiting a moment for someone else to say something in recognition of Ella's appearance or to suggest a new layout for our games since we are a group of seven, I try myself. "Do you play?" I ask, nudging the pool cue, unnecessarily, towards the tables.

Ella shakes her head, causing her light brown hair to swish around her head, and Lily supplies, "She just likes to cheer us on." The two girls share a small smile.

Simply accepting the answer, I move to break the game for Ivy and me. I fumble it slightly but get the balls spread out enough that I'm not ashamed of them seeing it. As I look up for Ivy to take the next shot, I see she is suddenly wearing a black cap and is pulling it low over her face with a serious expression as she studies the game. I have to laugh, Ivy's goofiness is always a highlight to my day.

As our game goes on, I realise Ivy is a good player, better than me, but not by so much it makes the game boring for me. Ivy is just lining up a shot for the black, she's potted everything else and I still have two reds to go, when I remember Ian's newfound liking of her and decide to make an attempt at wing-manning. Since I know I have no tact for this sort of thing, I go for the blunt method. "So, Ian likes you."

Ivy hits the ball at a far bigger angle than she should have been aiming for, and the two balls spiral all around the table while Ivy stands straight up and lifts her cap off her head, total rabbit in headlights. "What do you mean?" Her scared tone is something I associate more with Ella, who fears the modern world, than Ivy, who embraces it.

"He likes you." I say shrugging, my eyebrows furrowing as I wonder if, as was quite likely when in this house, I am missing something.

"Like a friend?" Asks Ivy, both worry and hope high in her voice.

Instead of answering I swither my head in mock consideration before gesturing with my right hand, rising it upwards in a 'more' motion.

Ivy immediately groans and does a little twirl of frustration, balling up her fists slightly as she does so.

"I'm guessing that's not a good thing." I say, wishing I hadn't said anything but also very happy I'd now be able to suggest Ian not act on his feelings.

Ivy shakes her head, more insistently than Ella had, her short violet hair bobbing around her face. Jade eyes glistening, instead of shining, like normal.

Behind me I hear a cue being placed down on a table and turn to see all the others watching our conversation, an array of mild concern and sympathy across their faces. Lily, like earlier, supplies reason for the other girls' behaviour. "Ivy doesn't date. Or…" She clarifies, possibly realising date is a more serious word for our generations courting process. "Anything like that. She's never had any interest."

I turn back to Ivy who looks a lot more worried than I feel necessary. "In guys, or in any kind of dating?" I ask, trying not to pry, but wanting to make sure I understand.

"Any kind, it's not who I am."

"Fair enough. Do you want me to subtly tell Ian that?" I shrug as I say it, unconcerned. Ian may like Ivy but I know him, he has no interest in going after someone who has no interest, no matter the reason, and they are friends anyway, if that's all they can be, it'll be all he wants.

From the tense atmosphere in the room and the stare Ivy gives me, I worry I've said the wrong thing, or misunderstood something. Before I start to apologise, Ivy dashes around to my side of our table and leaps forward to hug me. I have to drop my cue to catch her in time but I manage it, and hug her back, realising how much has changed since our first hug and my initial awkwardness.

As we both hold onto our hug and I feel the rest of the tension in the room dissipate, I see, out the corner of my eye, Danny continue with his game against Sam, and I try to make sense of the reason for Ivy's reaction. A wave of realisation rushes over me and I squeeze Ivy, even tighter, for a moment before she lets go. I may have no problem accepting her not wanting to date, but really that was a pretty new way of thinking, there are plenty of people my age who find different types of sexual and romantic orientation odd or simply fake. Being as old as they are must have meant living through all the ages of morality the world had lived through, many of which must have been crushing to comply yourself to, especially if they came after times of freedom. The people before me are not bound to reality but they live in it, I know from Sam, the regret they could feel for going along with history, and I realise now, from Ivy, the pain they themselves might have lived through for it.

Ivy goes back to our game, face shining, gesturing for me to take my turn and allow us to return to normalcy and I pick my cue up off the floor. I line up my shot and sink the red ball I aim for easily, smiling proudly at that. Trying to smother the pride I feel at being someone who's opinion Ivy does not need to worry about, and let us go back to just two friends playing a game.

For the next couple of games, I sit out, having lost to Ivy, and simply sit, in a chair matching Ella's, and joke with all the others. My chair is right next to Ella's and I enjoy the chance to talk to her normally, other times it has always been just the two of us and the air feels too charged, sitting here, everything relaxed, I get to see her just enjoying herself.

As we laugh at a particularly bad shot of Lily's who is incapable of putting any force on the ball, I watch Ella clutch at her stomach trying to restrain her laughter and I try to hold that image of her up against the mask of fear she'd worn before and during Ian's party. I had assumed Ella had a fear of the modern world, but the way she's talking and joking in here, doesn't seem in any way out of time. So, I start to wonder what she is afraid of.

When Ivy finishes her game against Cara, in a landslide victory, I again bear witness to her victory dance, this time actually deserved. From the look on her face I can guess Cara is picturing a violent attack via pool cue. It's meant to be Sam and I playing next, but I lean over to Ella instead. "Are you sure you won't play?"

Ella's eyes focus on me and I see a subtle shift in the ocean of blue there. "I'll try, but I'm awful."

Like with the party I am sure everyone else is shocked to see Ella picking up a cue and standing by the side of the table, but like they'd ended up doing then, they deal it with by not acknowledging it's happening. Like a gazelle at a watering hole, not that they were going to eat her. I set up the balls and again break the game, standing up I blow air dramatically out of my cheeks. "I'm awful too."

Now I will admit, Ella is bad. She plays like she'd never held a cue before, well she holds a cue like she'd never held a cue before. It's cute though, her look of concentration as she picks her shot and the crease in her forehead that appears every time the balls don't move the way she wants them to, it's all adorable and I slightly regret asking her to play. I'm not looking at her like a friend and it must be pretty obvious. Ivy's reaction to Ian liking her has lessened my desire to do anything in the near future about my feelings for Ella. My feelings however are not listening to the rest of me.

Somehow our game ends up with just the black left to pot and both of our concentration increases. I may be a good older brother to Katie, but I still play to win at Monopoly against her and the rest of my family, I take games a little too seriously. Ella also seems to have decided that if she is going to play a game of pool, she has to win it.

I have a clear shot of the black, which Ella has accidentally handed to me and as I lean over the table, I can almost feel her annoyance at being about to lose radiate out from her. Trying to ignore it and not be a soppy kid with a crush and throw the game for her, I go for my shot. Just before I make contact, I feel the subtle press of lips against my cheek, and my shot goes to hell, I mean, really, the white bounces off the table.

Standing up straight I whirl my head around, expecting to see Cara standing there, grinning mischievously like she does. Instead the only person by my side is Ella, her hands over her mouth, looking even more shocked than I do.

"I didn't mean to do that." She gasps out, removing her hands from her mouth just enough that I can make out her words.

Blinking wildly, I look between her and the table again, trying to get my head around what has just happened.

Ella rubs her face into her hands before speaking again, rambling. "I'm sorry, I just didn't want to lose and I get so competitive and I shouldn't have done that, I'm sorry."

"I didn't mind." I think I mean to say it in a blow off manner, like it doesn't matter, but my tone definitely portrays the real reason I hadn't minded.

Both mine and Ella's cheeks bloom red.

Looking around again, partly for a second of not looking at her, I want to double check none of the others had seen or heard what had just happened and been said, but I see that the room is empty. I hadn't realised the others had left, how immersed in our game had we been?

My hand lifts subconsciously to tug at the hair on the back of my neck while I try to fathom something to say, either to continue the moment we are still suspended in, or to pop the bubble and drop us back to Earth.

"I'm not like Ivy." Ella blurts.

I face her again. "What?"

"She's not with anyone because she doesn't want to be, I'm not like Ivy but I'm...it's..." Whether because she doesn't know what to say or how to say it, Ella's words trail off.

"So you want to?" I ask, tentatively trying the words out, pretty sure that's not what she is saying but hoping anyway.

"It's complicated. I'm...You really don't know me Will. Believe me, you don't want to." Ella is backing away awkwardly and I hate to see the fear back on her face, I hate it being there because of me.

"Ok, that's fine. Honestly. Please don't worry. We can forget it." I'm shaking my head and holding up my hands in a placating gesture. Wishing as I never thought I would, that she hadn't kissed me on the cheek.

Ella's eyes are so big as she looks into my own, exploring them for the truth in my words which I hope they find. As I am just beginning to properly see, these people are all complicated beneath their initial, perfect, outward images, and I can't even begin to guess at the reasons behind their actions. Like there's any way you could attempt using basic psychology on them. These people are made up of more history than anyone else I know, I don't need to know the particulars to know it is beyond me. Ella, understanding Ella, is beyond me, and I know it.

Eventually she relaxes again, and her blue eyes return to a normal size. "I'm sorry, again. But yes, can we forget it?"

I try not to let the words sting, but they do, they sting at my eyes and my chest. I meant what I said though and I could let what had just happened go, return to the way we'd smiled together from a small distance, watching a game of pool. Taking a breath, I move one of my raised hands to point at the pool table.

Attempting a joke, I ask, "Does that mean I won?"

CHAPTER 21

The past week has turned my world upside down and I've been clinging to the edge. Somehow my world has already started to feel normal again, I've adjusted, and I can finally let myself relax. Once I get back to my flat, I don't even bother to take my clothes off, or get under the covers. I just fall onto my bed and sleep.

When sunlight starts streaming through my windows, I open my eyes just enough to check my phone. I was meaning to check the time but instead see a text has arrived from Cara. I've apparently missed our lecture and our hand in by this time, but she is just letting me know she'd handled it. Without allowing my mind to start spinning about how she'd managed to text me without me having given her my number, or without having a real phone, I drop mine back to the floor and roll over to sleep some more.

By the time I wake up properly, enough to get myself out of a strictly horizontal position, the light outside is beginning to dim again. I smile at my window, oddly smug about my sloth-ish day, I have them so rarely.

Stumbling out of my bed to get some cereal, I realise I also slept in my shoes, making my smile grow, stupidly. Entering the kitchen, I wipe the grin of my face when I see Isaac, not wanting to explain the silly reason for it. Isaac looks up from his phone, I assume he is killing time while the oven behind him cooks his dinner for him. He is having dinner and I've just risen for the day.

"Ruffled clothes, bedhead and at six in the evening. Please

tell me the girl you like is in your room right now?" Isaac teases.

Self-consciously I raise my hand to my hair, he's right, from the feel of it, bedhead is the appropriate word. "No. Really no. I just had some serious sleep to catch up on." I yawn as I get the words out, still, somehow, not fully awake.

Isaac tilts his head at me. "You have been out a lot lately. Everything ok...family wise?"

I drop my hand from toying with my hair, caught a little short. I've never told Isaac about any of my family stuff, it isn't what we talk about. Then again, not talking about something doesn't stop it being obvious. "Yeah, that's fine. My plate just suddenly got quite full."

A timer goes off on Isaac's phone as he studies me. He jumps, lankily, and we don't say any more as he rushes around getting his food out the oven and dishing it up for himself, and also making up another plate.

I grin behind him, taking in what he is wearing and putting two and two together. "Nice clothes, fancy food and at six in the evening. Please tell me the guy you like is here?"

Even not facing me, Isaac's embarrassment is obvious. "Maybe."

"Good work." I say, my voice biting with happiness for him. Moving properly into the kitchen to start on my cereal, I let Isaac edge past me, balancing the two plates between his hands.

As he reaches the door and uses his back to prop it open, Isaac catches my eye. "You know I can try and help. With full plate stuff, whatever's on it."

I just smile and nod, letting Isaac duck out the room to his date. Normally I just think of him as a flatmate, someone who kept a tidy enough kitchen and doesn't make too much noise, it's nice to get a reminder that we are friends. Grabbing a bowl and filling it to the brim with cereal, the smile stays on my face.

I've left no room in the bowl for milk and grab the whole milk bottle along with a spoon as I head back to my room, I can eat some dry and then add milk as I get the space. Back in my room I flop down onto my bed to eat, I've covered my desk in books in an attempt to encourage later study but now is not the time, maybe later. The eternal state of my academic life, 'maybe later'.

Picking up my phone to settle into falling down a hole with Youtube videos while I eat, I see a screenful of notifications. A couple messages from Ian asking where I am and telling me where he is before he gave up on me responding, a photo from Jackie in our group chat which I'm sure would be an unflattering photo of someone at the lunch I missed, and lastly a number of missed calls from my mum. My mum calls a lot, so I don't worry at the number there are but when I see another missed call, this one from my Dad, I almost drop my phone in my rush to hit redial. My dad never just calls me.

"Katie's fine." My dad's voice answers as soon as he picks up. I almost collapse back in relief, my heart jumping painfully against my ribs. "Your mother thought me calling would get a reaction. I figured it wouldn't be a good one."

I fight the urge to agree using too much profanity. "Yeah, it wasn't."

A moment of silence I decide to take as amiable descends on the phone line. There is a reason my dad doesn't call, most of his communication lies in his presence, shifting his shoulders or making pointed glances, he is lost when just a voice.

"Was there a particular reason Mum wanted to talk to me?" I try to keep the annoyance out my voice since it isn't aimed at him.

"She just wanted a catch up and couldn't wait. I'd give you to her now but she'd giving Katie a bath."

I nod in reaction, you'd think I'd have to say something but I know my dad will be able to sense the movement. Before I have the chance to free him from the conversation, he speaks again. "What were you doing that you missed so many calls?" His tone isn't in any way reprimanding, simply curious. Normally I miss two calls, max.

"I was asleep, it's been a long week." My voice grows tired again as I say it and I rub restlessly at my eyes. "Sorry I should've responded."

"No, it's good. Taking some time. Being a little selfish when you need it, it's good. We never taught you that." Again, his voice isn't negative in any way, there is no bitterness, just surprise with a glimmer of pride.

I don't respond, that time because I don't know what to say. My mouth hangs open as I hold onto the phone, trying to move my mouth into the shape of what I want to say. That they have taught me everything important, that I don't mind not having the time to be selfish, that I love what our family is. It feels like making too big of a deal of his words to say any of that, and to not say anything feels too small. I stay silent and feel the meaning travel through the line anyway.

"Have a good night." Says my dad, ending the connection.

I drop my phone back down and begin to absentmindedly spoon my dry cereal into my mouth. I feel suddenly wrapped up in the people of my life, cocooned by them. The humans of my life. Isaac and my dad, usually both background figures to the rest of my life are still there for me. It isn't necessarily a surprise, especially when it comes to my dad, but having a confirmation feels pretty damn good.

CHAPTER 22

The rest of that night is spent sprawled across my bed reading textbooks and making notes for different assignments. There is something peaceful about a whole day spent on normal things, food, sleep and work. No others.

I expect to find it difficult to get to sleep once night time crawls around again but it isn't, possibly aided by the fact I am actually under the covers and dressed for sleep.

The next morning is a Thursday, a day I luckily have no classes, though I had inadvertently had none the day before either. I make myself another bowl of cereal and have a small talk with Eric, my other flatmate in the kitchen as I eat, Isaac doesn't appear so I have no chance to find out how his date had gone. After checking with Eric that he doesn't mind me taking over the bathroom, I have a long shower, stretching out my muscles as I clean them, standing under the spray of hot water with my face towards the stream for several minutes, enjoying not thinking.

I pack my backpack with all my textbooks and set off to get a bus back to my parent's, thinking it is a good time to give my mum the catch up she wants and missing spending time with Katie, regretting she hasn't been the main thing on my mind. My brain has taken a break from asking questions about Cara, Lily, Danny, Sam and all the rest, they are my friends, I don't have to stress about who they are beyond that. Watching the streets roll past out the bus window, I lean my head against the cool glass, I have bigger things to worry about and there is no question of that now.

When I get to the house, I ring the doorbell instead of letting myself in, allowing my mum to open the door to me and pull me inside, instantly complaining about my lack of communication. If I let myself in, she would've been deprived of the cathartic pleasure of dragging me inside. Dropping my bag to the floor I let her words wash over me, about her shopping and daily chores that she finds just as boring as I do.

My mum leads me into the living room and I instantly move over to were Katie sits wrapped up in what looks like a dozen blankets. I lift her small body up and plop her and her nest onto my lap, kissing her forehead. Katie doesn't respond, except to grab at my arm and pull it around her. My mum doesn't stop talking and just keeps drivelling on while she straightens blankets and books on the coffee table and everything else that doesn't need straightened. There may be nothing pressing she wants to talk about, but sometimes my mum just needs to talk. Anything is better than standing still and silent.

Despite all the blankets Katie feels cold in my arms and I wrap them tighter around her like that will do anything. Her eyes are on the tv and though she doesn't seem to be watching it that intently I let it play. After treatments Katie can feel nauseous for days, and it helps her to concentrate on one spot. We normally make it the tv so she can pretend to watch, she doesn't like acknowledging she feels sick. She is our warrior.

Along with my bag of books, I'd brought my mum a massive stack of unwashed clothes and she starts in on washing them straight away, changing her topic of chatter to how I should look after myself better. It is a monologue she's perfected but I know she prefers to deliver it than to have me listen. She needs to act like a normal mum, take care of her kids and lecture them.

Somewhere upstairs I can hear my dad moving around, probably working at the mini office he's stuck in the corner of my parent's bedroom. Katie stares, my mum paces, my dad goes upstairs and I just show up when I can. That's how treatment days work. There isn't exactly comfort we find in this routine of ours but it's better than no routine.

I could've told a story and tried to distract Katie, but that might distract her from her spot, so I stay silent. Slowly moving to unzip my bag I pick up one of my textbooks and rest it on the arm of the sofa, keeping my other arm around Katie while I start to read.

Every time the programme on screen changes to something too boring or depressing, I change channels to something with at least a little humour in it. When I get bored of a book I switch over to another topic and keep going, all the while paying close attention to jostling Katie as little as possible.

When the time comes around for lunch and dinner I eat in the kitchen with my parent's. The smell of any food makes Katie gag, so we make sure to keep it away from her.

The silence of the house, once my mum gives up on her rambling, is so loud. Like an elephant bustling around every room, trying to be noticed. We know the elephant and are very familiar with it, but give no acknowledgement of its presence. There is a little girl staring at a spot on our tv, that is all that is important just now, everything else is moot and will remain mute.

Eventually, when darkness falls outside and Katie's eyes begin to droop, I take the cue from my parents pointed looks between her and me, and carry her upstairs. Sometimes Katie fights being carried around on days like these, it hurts the image she has of herself as a warrior. I hope she will discover she can be our warrior without having to ignore needing help.

Today, she doesn't argue, some of the fight seems to have gone out of her, more than she normally allows. I try not to squeeze her too tightly through all her blankets and instead attempt to twist my thoughts into a story for her, something to brighten the thunder clouds over her head and the shadows under her eyes.

Recently all my stories have been about the Gods, making them pixies, or witches, or any kind of magical creature, Katie's lapped them all up. My mind is, however, for the first time, blanking on how to translate them into fiction. My world of fake has become too real, they have become too real to me.

Once I get Katie into her bed and kneel by her bedside, I silently pick up Winston and move him over to her, mimicking galloping. Silence is an odd thing between me and my sister, they are normally used as dramatic pauses, rather than awkward ellipses. As her little arm stretches out for Winston, her hand finds mine as well and she holds on tight.

I stay there, holding her hand, a toy dog between us, for hours, resting on my knees and never moving, even when they become numb and pins and needles creep over my whole body. The strength in her hand is all I need in the whole world, and as I watch over her delicate sleeping frame, it finally settles in my mind, the fact that one day she will be gone.

And that it might kill me.

CHAPTER 23

Somehow my body falls into sleep, and I wake up hours later, still being clung to by Katie's warm hand, with a blanket slung over my shoulders. I smile softly as I blink the sleep from my eyes, the work of my mother.

Seeing the beginning of sunlight radiating through Katie's pink flowery curtains I finally move my hand out of hers and rise to leave her room. Whether to go to my own room and sleep or go downstairs and block out my brain with old sitcoms on the tv, I'm not sure.

As usual of late, the decision is made for me.

Cara stands on the landing, just outside Katie's room, leaning on the banister on her elbows, facing me dead on. If I go into my room I know she'll follow, same goes for the living room, I stalk past her down the stairs anyway, figuring somewhere there lays my best option for ditching her.

The whole house is quiet, so I am relieved that Cara keeps her voice low as she follows me. "No need to act coy, I'm just checking up on you."

"I don't need checking up on." I don't quite manage to whisper back, an edge in my voice I hate being there.

I can feel Cara's eye roll behind my head. "We haven't heard anything from you since playing pool and Sam telling you about his scar."

Had those two things really been on the same day? Time never seems to work in my head where they are concerned. "That was only two days ago."

"You skipped class."

"I skipped one day, everyone skips days."

"You're not everyone."

We've reached the bottom of the stairs and are moving through the hallway, but I spin around at her words. I hate there being so many expectations of me. I'm a good guy, I treat people nicely, I keep my head above water with all the shit going on in my life. I can't stand that that means I'm not allowed a day off. My dad's words about it being good to be a little selfish have been ringing around my brain since he said them.

"I just needed-" I cut myself off, my voice had been too loud, I don't want to wake anyone. "I just needed a couple days focussing on my real life." I finish, back to whispering. Family and university, that's all I have the head space for, focussing on anything, anyone, else takes away from that.

"We're part of your life." Cara says, meeting my angry gaze with a fire burning in her own eyes, hurt mingling in her tone.

I exhale and break our little staring match, raking my hands through my hair and leaning my shoulder against the wall to my right. "I know. I just can't, Cara."

The fire in her eyes sparks. "So, Ella tells you she can't do a relationship and you dump all of us?"

I just look at her for a moment, lost in how to explain that's not true. "No, it's what all of you said that day. Everything you let me in on, about all of you, it shows how old you are, how much you've lived through. I'm living through enough, I can't take on anymore."

"We're not asking you to *take us on*," Says Cara, showing exactly how stupid she thinks my comment is. "We're just letting you know, you wanted us to explain and we can stop if you want, but you're the one that asked." Bitterness laces her words.

"Then stop. I don't not want to know you, but I can barely

handle what I do know." I gesture my hand up the stairs towards Katie, trying to explain with my eyes why I'm done. I'd asked to know if they could help her, along the way I'd become their friends and that wasn't going to change. But I don't see the point in learning about Gods when they can't do anything real.

Cara relents, I can see it happen in her eyes. "Ok." The word hangs in the air between us, almost tangible as I try to figure out what to do next.

She decides, like usual, for me. "Go upstairs and get some sleep. I'll leave you alone." Cara turns right on her heal after saying it, and her red hair swishes out around her.

As she opens the door to leave, I can't stop myself asking a question before I head upstairs. "Did you put the blanket over me?" I'm unsure what makes me ask or think to ask.

Cara stops in the doorway and I see her shoulders rise in a deep breath before she turns back to me. "Thought you were going to stop with your questions. You didn't like the answers."

I just shrug, maybe my brain loves to torture itself with more than it can handle.

"Yes Will, I put the blanket over you. You looked cold." Cara says it gently and lets the door swing shut a moment later. Slamming in the distance and silence between us.

CHAPTER 24

I stand staring at the closed door. I've never heard Cara speak softly without there being a tease of flirting or general messing with someone involved. I'd also never expected a simple kind gesture from her, the others yes, but not Cara.

Shaking my head out of the moment, I trudge upstairs. Trying to fight all the questions her act springs up in my mind. I can't handle them. They are a great distraction, but I can't help thinking they did too good a job of distracting me.

I only get a couple more hours sleep in bed before my mum wakes me up for breakfast. When I stumble back down the stairs after a quick shower, I expect to see Katie back in front of the tv but she isn't there. My dad stops me before I head right back upstairs to see if she's still in her room.

"She's outside, wanted to sunbathe she said." He says it from the kitchen table, where he's doing the puzzles in the paper. Picking at his breakfast of porridge. He hates porridge but my mum always insists he hasn't given it enough of a shot, and has been insisting this for at least a decade.

Grabbing myself some cereal, I take the bowl right out into the back garden, sitting myself down cross legged in my pyjama trousers. "Hey Kit Kat." I say, peering over her. She's freed herself of the blankets from yesterday and lies down in the grass wearing just her cosy pyjamas and slippers, with Winston clutched to her stomach.

"Shh." Whispers Katie, not looking at me, as she scans the overgrown greenery of our little garden.

Though I am pleased she is apparently feeling a lot better

144

than yesterday, I can't help my astonishment that I've just been shushed, she never shushes me.

"Kate?" I whisper back, only allowing myself one syllable of speech, a little worried by the intensity of her concentration, on nothing.

"Shhh, Will look."

Forgetting the cereal in my lap I look around with her, trying to get myself into her world, but I don't see anything.

Without warning, Katie sits up and my cereal almost crashes over both of us as I reach out instinctually, to help her, sure she'll make herself dizzy or nauseous again. However, she looks completely fine as her face shines, looking towards my mother's attempt at a rose bush that rests next to our door, right behind me.

As I turn, I catch sight of violet in my periphery. I whip my head around to see what it is but don't see anything. Katie giggles at me, and I swivel my head back to her. "What?"

"She's too fast for you." Katie giggles again, her big eyes still shining.

My eyebrows crease together, and I begin to look around the garden again, suspicion niggling up the back of my neck.

Katie squeals and starts pointing again, but this time I see it too, a streak of purple glimmer flits through my vision by another bush in our garden. An inkling of what is going on, blossoms in my chest as I loose sight of it again.

"It's a fairy." Says Katie, in hushed tones full of delight.

I smile back at her. "Yeah it looks like one."

"You said it's really lucky to see one."

"It is, you're really lucky." My voice chokes a little on the last word and I can feel my eyes beginning to water.

Just in time however my dad comes into the garden. I swear he is reading my mind this morning. "Katie, come on inside. Try and have a little breakfast."

Katie groans, but allows our dad to slowly shuffle her indoors, she hates trying to eat until she is a few days passed treatment, it always comes right back up, or she feels like it is on the edge of doing so, for hours.

I stay in the garden, nonchalantly beginning to spoon my now mushy cereal into my mouth. It's only once I hear Katie arguing about which breakfast foods she will and will not try, that I speak into the empty space. "Ivy?"

And there she is, sitting cross legged right in front of me, in her cropped haired pixie look. "Hey Will." She chirps happily. I don't even flinch.

"What are you doing here?" I ask, no irritation in my voice, but simple curiosity as to why she is there.

"Hanging with Katie."

"Is this the first time you've been hanging out with her?" I ask, scooping more cereal into my mouth.

"No, it's like the second or third time." There is no apology in Ivy's voice, just her normal buzz.

Shaking my head, I fight how to feel about Ivy pretending to be a fairy for my sister. Some part of me wants to feel angry about it, but I can't get a handle on why, the rest of me is remembering the look of sheer joy on Katie's face. "Thank you."

Ivy shrugs and tucks up her knees so she can hug them, her bright jade eyes pouring into mine. We sit for a long moment like that, her just looking at me and me scraping out the last of my cereal, running out of reasons not to look at her. She breaks our silence. "I'm sorry we were too much."

My eyes sting again, I drop my bowl onto the grass and rub at my eyes with the base of my palms. "It's everything else that's too much."

Though I don't hear her move, I'm not startled when I feel Ivy's hands on my shoulders. "I know." She isn't agreeing with what I'm saying, I can tell, she is understanding how I feel.

As I almost allow myself to slip into her embrace, the reason for my earlier anger becomes clear to me. "Why can you make her feel better?" I ask bitterly, releasing my face from my hands to look at her imploringly.

Ivy's eyes brim with tears. "I thought that's what you wanted?"

I fight my mind again for the reason behind my feelings. "I wanted you to make her *be* better, not just feel better." Some part of my brain knows being angry about making her feel better holds little sense, but that doesn't stop me feeling it.

"But this is all we can do. I told you before, we can help, we can ease the load, but we can't take anything away."

"Then what's the point?!"

"You know the point!"

We've begun shouting again, I don't even care if my parents hear us. Ivy's eyes are imploring now, begging me to hear what she is saying.

Somewhere along our bickering I'd risen up onto my knees, I slump back down. I do know the point, it's the whole point to my life. Getting Katie to laugh or just smile and forget, for however long I can manage, that her life isn't fair. The parts of me that I hate, hate the fact that Ivy can do that better than me.

Katie hadn't even winced when she'd sprung up to catch sight of her fairy, and it was only the second day after her treatment. And the look on her face, she smiles and laughs for me, but her joy is never that pure.

Getting myself a bit more together, I nod at Ivy and rub at my eyes again. Feeling apologetic but also just wanting to get away from Ivy and all the mixed feelings the whole lot of them brought to my life.

I grab my empty bowl from the ground after another moment and stand, readying myself to head inside and probably explain to my parents the reason for my earlier yelling. Ivy doesn't try and stop me, she stays sprawled on the grass, looking so grey despite her usual brightly coloured outfit. I turn away from her, away from feeling bad for dulling her rainbow, which doesn't work.

Back inside the house, I find Katie sat at the table with lots of different breakfast foods surrounding her, grimacing at them each in turn. Our parents sit either side of her, trying to encourage eating while also acting nonchalant, making for an awkward little panto. They don't even look up as I come in, they hadn't heard my yelling, when you are in the bubble of worrying over Katie, everything else stops registering. For the first time that thought brings up of a bubble of a silenced scream in my throat that I long to pop.

I gulp it down and instead join them all at the table. "Kid, you gotta eat that one before Dad gets to it, his belt can't take it." I joke, pointing at a tub of yogurt and granola and glancing dramatically towards our dad's only slightly bulging stomach.

Going along with my mockery as he can only bring himself to do on days like these, my dad licks his lips and rubs his hands together. Overacting by my standards, but enough to make Katie giggle and tentatively reach for a spoon. I know the cold of the yogurt will ease the dryness in her throat she refuses to admit to having.

We all stay around the table, and as Katie's miniscule spoonful's slow on the way to her mouth we all pick up our own spoons and help her finish. We must look like a bizarre game of hungry hippos, which me and my mum play into especially and start making exaggerated gulping noises. Katie laughs and clutches her stomach, I know in part because her stomach is churning, but at least we give her an excuse.

After enough time that her stomach can settle, I return Katie to the sofa and to staring at her spot. While I gather her up in my arms my mum reminds me not to miss my classes, I splutter for a moment before realising she is talking about my afternoon tutorial later today, not my missed classes of the day before.

Every so often Katie tilts her head a little away from her spot to catch me in her periphery and asks questions about her fairy sighting. I kiss the top of her head after each question and answer them the best I can. My heart aching for what Ivy has done for Katie, and my eyes stinging yet again for still feeling angry about it.

CHAPTER 25

Days pass until Tuesday rolls back around, with part of me dreading going into English. Wishing somehow that my life will go back to normal and I'll just be able to sit with my human friends. I wince as the thought passes through my mind, but that doesn't make it less real.

I walk apprehensively through the double doors into the lecture theatre but have no need to worry. Ian and Jack sit alone, laughing at something on Ian's phone. Walking over to them, I allow myself to smile and flop into my seat next to them.

For the first time in what feels like a long time, I listen to everything my lecturer says and take proper notes of everything, even allowing Ian to doodle a rocket on the corner of my page when he gets bored. Ian's notebook is so full of sketches he looks like an art student, one without talent. I smirk down at my book when I see he's also drawn a little planet for the rocket to head to, with a tiny flag labelled 'boredom', he may have no artistic talent, but it's funny. To me at least. I find myself imagining the unamused look on Cara's face if she saw the drawing, and quickly try to squash the thought.

I get through History as well with no problems, then as we head out the class and discuss plans for lunch, with Ian interjecting gossip about our friends from the weekend and Jack snorts, I can't stop myself from asking.

"Is Ivy joining us again?"

Ian and Jack blink at me, confused. "Ivy?" Asks Jack, speaking up for both of them.

I laugh confusedly. "You know Ivy, cool girl, been hanging out with us since your birthday." I say, gesturing with my head towards Ian.

He smiles at me, still looking confused but it mingles with indulgence, raising a hand to pat my shoulder. "Will, this daydreaming of yours is too much. We've not started hanging out with anyone new in ages, and the girls we hang out with are only semi-cool."

I shrug his patronising hand off me, and my eyebrows knit together as I stare at him, trying to decipher something in his face showing he is kidding. There isn't anything. He just laughs at my face, obviously convinced I am making a bad joke, and deciding to find it funny.

We continue on our way to lunch, with Jack and Ian continuing to catch me up on their weekends like I'm not acting weird. I try to listen to them but am too lost in my haze of confusion. Taking my mind back to the lecture I visualise everything I'd seen in the room, trying to remember if I'd caught sight of Cara there, but I'd been trying so hard not see her, I have no clue if she was there.

Once we are sat down at our table, I fight the urge to ask them about Cara, worried they'll look at me like I've grown a second head again. I settle on trying another tactic as I take out the box of leftovers, one of many that my mother forced on me, days ago. "Do you think Lucas Emerson will ever be able to hold himself back from staring at the hot girl in our class? He's got to be dropping his grade with every glance at her." It is a crass way to bring up the suggestion of Cara, but Lucas is known to be annoying, so I am bound to have some of my friends find it funny.

Sure enough, Jack laughs into his bottle of coke, almost choking. Jackie speaks up as she claps him on the back. "Will, don't refer to someone as 'hot girl'."

Ian defends me from Jack's other side. "To be fair there

are at least three Chloes in our class, 'hot girl' is an easy identifier. Plus, there is no way Lucas is passing English anyway, so who cares."

A few people at our table laugh again, with Jack being able not to choke again, in doing so. I smirk and stare down at my food, the bite I've just taken feeling too dry in my mouth. There is no way Ian wouldn't label Cara as the hot girl over Chloe, or forget who Ivy was.

I try not to think about it, them, I go to the library before my last class and start typing up drafts of the assignments, I've made notes on at home. I go to my Philosophy lecture and grab a coffee with Ian afterwards, we're skipping football this week because Ian is crying pulled muscle. All I can think while we chat over our drinks is the fact he doesn't know Cara and Ivy anymore. I even try talking about his party and he briefly comments on him and I getting a taxi to the hospital before sleeping at mine.

It's no good. I head straight from our café to that old Victorian house, needing an explanation though I know I don't deserve one after how I left it with Cara and Ivy. Outside the house, I pace along the brick wall outside for a while before entering the gate, and then I pace up and down the small path before I make it right up to the door. Spotting a doorbell, I've never noticed before, I ring it and anxiously wait, wanting to pace some more.

An old man opens the door, peering at me over reading glasses, a paper held in the hand not holding open the door. "Hello?" He asks in a quaveringly unsure voice.

Taking in his appearance, I gaze into his eyes, half expecting, hoping, them to be jade green and Ivy to be messing with me. Instead I see pale brown, watery eyes, and can make out a regular hallway in the space behind him.

I take a step back and absent-mindedly look up and down the street, checking I've got the right door. The old man closes the door a little more, but keeps looking at me, his eyes concerned. "Are you alright?"

Looking back at him, I shake my head back into reality. "I'm sorry. Yes. wrong door. Didn't mean to bother you."

I turn to retreat back down the steps but can't bring myself to descend them, I'm frozen on the boundary of something. Of what I'm not sure.

The door behind me doesn't shut right away. "Go home, boy." I hear the man say as the door finally moves to creak shut.

It's just a hint, a sliver of disdain in the man's words that make me twist and hold the door, just a fraction open. "Danny?"

I almost fall forward as the door opens fully, but I manage to only stumble for a moment. The hallway I'd glimpsed remains, but the old man has blinked into Danny, full black attire and all. "Well, I can remove stupid from the list of reasons you annoy me. Or at least lower its importance."

We glare at each other, I've never noticed that his eyes are dark enough to match his wardrobe before, but there is such a lack of colour anywhere in his eyes, just a monochrome contrast. Maybe they aren't always like that and he's doing it for effect. If so, it is working, he looks less human than I'd seen any of their group, including when Ivy had been a cat.

"I want to see Cara." There is no chance I am talking to him while he's looking at me like that, and Cara seems more likely to be behind what the hell is going on with my friends than Ivy or the others.

Danny just tilts his head at me, with the black in his eyes seeming to grow, the change makes him look almost alien. I'm a second from running out the house when a hand appears on Danny's shoulder. In an instant his eyes are back to a human level of dark iris, and he moves aside to allow Cara to be visible. Without another word or a backward glance, he leaves through a door in the hallway, seeming wholly unbothered.

With a quick shake of my head I try to knock the shivering from my bones and focus on Cara instead. "What's going on?"

Cara sighs in both tiredness and irritation. "Will, you made it quite obvious you'd like us to leave to you alone. We are."

"That's not what I said."

"We inferred quite easily." The hurt in Cara's tone makes me look towards her shoes rather than her face. She wears simple white flats along with cropped blue jeans and a plain red top made of some light weight material, something about the outfit makes Cara look softer around the edges, less capable of attack at any instant. Everything reminds me that I'd been the more biting one of the two of us in our last conversation.

"I'm sorry."

Cara moves towards me and I find my eyes being pulled back up to her face. Her own eyes crackle with a fire I've never seen on her before, but the one I've seen a hundred times in Katie's eyes, the fire of trying to be strong. "We know, but we don't deserve to be pushed aside. If you can't handle who we are, then you can't have us."

The way she phrases it, like I'd had any kind of possession of them feels like a strike to my back, jerking me out of my own perspective. "It's what you are, not who." I attempt to argue, my voice small, even in the small space. But I can still hear the lie in it, the refusal to accept how intermingled those two things are. It's the things that I understand of what they are that has allowed me to be their friends. They can get along with other people, Danny can mess with Ian, Cara can tease Jack and Ivy can talk about boys with Jackie but that isn't friendship, not really. All the moments of friendship and connection I'd felt from other people, Ian, Isaac, my dad, they all came from understanding what I'm going through, mostly with Katie, understanding what is important to me.

I think of clasping Sam's hand after he showed me a fraction of his story, Ivy hugging me tightly for not questioning her lack of care for relationships and Ella's hand and mine tightening over each other to comfort without need for words. Without having access to what all of them are I wouldn't have been capable of those moments, and I wouldn't trade those moments for anything, even peace.

"I don't know what to do." I say, speaking up from my silence.

Cara laughs, the sound resonating with the condescension I usually associate with her. "Stop fighting us. Give up a little control."

I want to argue, feeling I've had no control since meeting any of them, but I hold my tongue, knowing she certainly has a point about fighting them. I settle for nodding instead.

Cara does a singular nod of her own head, and as she does so, the cramped hallway we've been standing in becomes again, the monstrous expanse of white wall I am used to. I barely scrunch up my eyes in response, apparently, I am getting the hang of the shifts in light that come with Cara's dramatic presence.

She is smiling at me now, holding her hands behind her back and twisting her body at the hips, when the doors around us begin to open and all the others appear. Sam, Lily and Ivy all walk right over to stand alongside Cara, while Danny stays stubbornly in his doorway, arms folded, and Ella stands somewhere in between, seeming to think I need space. I hate every inch she keeps away from me, sure I've put them there by staying away, after her lips had grazed my cheek. I need to find a time to explain how little that had had to do with her.

I smile around at all of them, trying to make it appear warm while also holding an apology for 'fighting' them.

"So," Ivy begins, bending forward at the waist slowly as

she speaks and springing back to upright as she continues, "You're going to let us properly be your friends and help?" Her words hold only excited hope, no reproach, and I am glad of it.

My smile stretches into a rueful grin. "I'm going to let you try."

CHAPTER 26

I get back to my flat that night feeling a little like I've been in court. We'd debated and organised how much they could be involved in my life, which was a truly odd experience. Leaning forward onto the large wooden table with a matching set of chairs that Cara, in her infinite whit, had drawn up for our meeting, and trying to explain the limits I needed in place, in order to let them do anything.

Don't be too obvious. That had been the main one. Katie may still be innocent enough to believe in fairies, but that came from a necessity to still believe in something. Even she wouldn't be able to take it if magic was suddenly surrounding her. Cara had started to argue about my calling them magic, but Lily had gently shushed her.

They'd asked me to explain Katie to them, and I had. Talking about my little sister was the easiest thing in the world to me and I hadn't held back. I told stories about her until my throat ran dry. Looking back up at them all after I'd finished and descended back into the present with them, I'd seen the oddest looks across all their faces. Remembering that we were focussing on Katie I hadn't asked, but I felt the time was coming that the previous humans of their life, and what had happened to them, would need to be discussed.

Anyway, in the end we didn't really know how to approach a solid plan on how I'd let them help Katie, it was too hard to predict. It was like a stab to my heart every time I thought that; how much worse she could be so soon, how much more pain she could be in. There had been moments when I just allowed myself to flit out of the conversation with them to focus on my breathing. Whenever I went back into the bubble of discussion with them, Ella's eyes were always on me, checking on me, even when the others were all distracted.

We decided that I would stay open with them as things progressed and eventually let them step in more. When she was worse, we never said it, but we all knew. They would be needed when she was worse, when nothing natural on our world could halt the pain of her dragging air into her lungs or of being dehydrated but unable to take a sip of water. The image both froze and burned my mind, it was like when you touch something just too cold out of the freezer and you can't hold onto it. The image came, it burned, and I dropped it quickly.

When we'd agreed on our plan of not really having a plan, I'd wanted to start attempting to change the conversation, lighten the mood. Ella had instead spoken up and asked about my parents and how they could help them. The others nodded along as if that was the next item on the agenda, but I'd shaken my head in surprise, having expected no help in the pain of the rest of us.

In the end I'd felt my brain sag from thinking about so many things I would rather not think about, and from the tiredness that seemed to keep sneaking up on me and offered to go home and talk to them the next day.

I get home just as Isaac is heading out, he is locking the door a I walk up the steps to it. Looking up at my approach, he grins through his mop of blond hair and in mock exasperation quickly unlocks the door for me.

"Hot date?" I ask, moving passed him into the doorway so I can shrug off my jacket. He is wearing a nice dark blue shirt paired with black trousers I've only seen him wear when he went on a job interview once. He didn't get the job,

Isaac's constant movement tends to make him look untrust-worthy to proper grown-ups.

"Hot *double* date." Isaac corrects, still grinning ear to ear. "I'm being introduced to the friends."

I chuckle at his obvious glee. "Ooh very serious." I mock, starting to turn into our flat and raising my hand to hide the yawn that rises in my throat.

Isaac reaches his arm out and pats my shoulder before he grabs the edge of the door to shut it again. "Get some sleep, mate."

Nodding despite the fact he can't see me, I head right for my room and change into some pyjamas at the bottom of one of my drawers. I set my alarm for the next morning and just close my eyes, hoping I'll find my way to sleep quickly.

Hours later, I'm more tired than I've felt in years and still unable to sleep. Watching the shadows creep over my ceil-ing, despising every inch of light that makes its way into my room and is keeping me awake. I've tried every possible position on my bed and even got up a while ago to do a little workout to tire my body out, like my mind. I only managed a couple push ups before giving up and crawling back into bed, amazed at my own lack of fitness.

My phone sits on the small table at the head of my bed, but I refuse to look at it, sure the glaring screen isn't going to help me sleep any more than anything else is. I click my alarm off, there's no point pretending I'm making my early class tomorrow. While I stare at the shadows, I try to think of nothing, then try to think of why I'm still awake, then try to imagine waves crashing against the beach. Nothing. My whole mind and body feel soaked in the stuff of sleep, but I still can't get to the point of switching off.

Giving up, I get up and go through to the kitchen. I slowly fill up the sink and started doing the dishes, trying to avoid making more noise than necessary and waking Eric. Finding rhythm in the labour I keep cleaning even after all the dirty dishes are washed. I take out the microwave plate and begin scrubbing it, vaguely aware of how disgusting we are to clean it so rarely.

I don't notice Isaac come back, not until he places his hand on my shoulder to halt my scrubbing. "Will?" His whispered voice isn't quite concerned, just sympathetic.

As I swivel my head towards him, I see the guy he'd held the door open for a wee while ago. He smiles passively at me from the doorway, hands in the pockets of his jeans, he wears a blazer, making him look a little smarter than the average student. My eyes meet Isaac's and I open my mouth to joke about dragging him from his date, but I can't get the words out.

"I know mate." Isaac says, still in his sympathetic tone, leading me by the shoulder he still holds, back to my room and easing me into bed.

"Is this where you make a gay joke?" I manage to get out, slurring slightly in my sleepy haze.

"This is where I tell you about my fabulous night out in such excruciating detail that you are bored to sleep." Isaac replies, moving his lanky frame to rest sitting on my floor.

I move to sit back up, to tell him it isn't necessary and it's late and that he has better things to do. But he just holds up his hand to stop me and begins talking. He describes every detail of the night, not in a lively way like I might tell Katie a story, but in a straight forward manner, saying 'and then... and then...and then'. The words quickly start to wash over me and lose all meaning, becoming only rhythm. Within minutes sleep finally gets me in an embrace.

CHAPTER 27

When I wake up, there's a puddle of drool all around the bottom of my face, I lean up on one arm to wipe it away, wiping at the sleep in my eyes at the same time. While I come out of the cocoon of sleep, I keep my hand over my eyes embarrassed that Isaac had had to take care of me. We're just flatmates, we help each other clean the bathroom or sort recycling, that's it, I need to apologise.

Stumbling out of bed I make my way straight for the kitchen, wanting to wolf down as much food as I can find in my sparse cupboards. I've just pushed the door open when I halt, a little awkwardly, catching sight of Ian who is sitting up on the counter flicking through a student cook book of Eric's. He looks up at my bumbling entrance, tossing the book down and pushing himself back into a standing position.

"Isaac texted me." He says, before I can ask. He's apparently skipping class too.

I rub at my eyes again and let out a groan, before I move passed him and pick up the book to put it back in its place. Eric gets quite fussy if we move his stuff, but hates confrontation enough he never says it.

When Ian realises I'm not about to start talking he does. "You've got to start taking better care of yourself. You're always good for like a week at a time and then you crash, there's got to be a better balance."

I hang my head. "I know."

"Knowing it isn't doing it, Will."

I raise my head back up and then lean it back to stare at the ceiling. I know that to, but saying it won't help right now. Ian is on the war path.

"If you need a hand, I could help out more, take some of the load. I love the kid too, you know that." Ian's voice is imploring with just a little crack in it at the end. He does, he was there before she was born and spoke to my mum's stomach as much as I did, trying to prepare her for the world. I don't really understand why I can't just turn around and tell him that yes, some help would be great, why I can't say that to everyone, but I just can't will myself to do it.

Instead, I turn towards him and grab him in a hug. Me and Ian don't hug much, we're close but we're not huggers. Except sometimes, when words fail, it's all we've got. Ian knows that and grips me tightly back, I feel his head shake as it rests on shoulder and grin to myself.

As I let him go, I can't handle another deep conversation, so I start a conversation I know he can't resist. "About Ivy." I'm fairly sure he's back to remembering who she, and the others are.

Ian's eyebrows instantly rise. "Yeah?" He definitely knows who she is.

Moving one of my hand's up I pat him on the shoulder and say, "She's ace, dude." I never call Ian 'dude' but sometimes it just feels necessary.

His shoulder slumps slightly against my hand and his eyes widen for a moment before he grins. "Good timing in telling me."

I feel my eyes slide together in confusion as I try to detect whether he's being sarcastic or not. What's he done? "Why?"

"She's coming round. Could've been awkward." He's laughing now, I realise it's in relief that I told him before he made any kind of move.

"What? You invited her round?" I shouldn't be as surprised as I am, he'd been called here after all, and it had probably seemed like a good opportunity for him to look good, being the supportive friend.

Ian just grins, and timed so perfectly I wonder if Ivy knew, the doorbell suddenly rings through the flat. Still grinning, he dodges out of my reach and through the door to let her in.

I'm about to start my search of the cupboards when I remember I'm wearing pyjamas, I'm quite sure Ivy does not remotely care what I wear, but I still feel the need to be dressed so I dive back into my room. My clothes from last night are lying tossed on the floor and I grab my jeans back up, not feeling the need for fresh ones. As I pull off my sleepwear, I pull open my top dresser drawer and stare at the shirts I have available, everything I wear is pretty basic so I don't understand how I take any time in choosing which thing to wear. I hear Ian and Ivy walking through the corridor to meet me in the kitchen, I don't want to give them any waiting time so grab any shirt and am still pulling it on as I open my room's door, checking that my fly is done up before I open the other door.

Ivy is perched on the counter exactly as Ian was, making me smile immediately, knowing they can't be a couple, I'm glad they're going to be so in sync as friends. Her trade mark orange docs are bouncing against the lower cupboards, she's got on a denim skirt and a multi-coloured fluffy jumper which is so big it's enveloping her. Ian who is standing opposite her is obviously trying not to look at her bare tan legs and I have to repress a laugh, he has only been given about a minute to start, not thinking about her like that. I pass them and finally open up my cupboard to see what food I've got. 'Sparse' was being kind earlier, I have an open jar of pasta sauce and a mostly eaten pack of chocolate covered biscuits. I grab the biscuits and lean against the counter too.

"So any plans for cheering me up?" I say, trying to sound light as I shove a biscuit in my mouth, chewing through its staleness.

Ivy literally claps her hands together as she bursts to tell me. "We're going to have a picnic!"

I frown at her, hoping it's not noticeable with my still full mouth. I swallow down most of the crumbs. "Outside? The weather is meant to be awful this weekend."

Ian pipes up. "It was when I was heading over, really windy, but Ivy said it's cleared up now.

Turning towards her I see a mischievous glint in her glowing green eyes and realise that the weather may be awful, but it won't be awful for us. I relent and grin at her. "Ok then, picnic sounds fun. Are we thinking George fifth's?" It's a park pretty near my flat, it's got lots of playground areas for different kid ages but there's a massive grassy area for dog walkers and I guess picnics.

Ivy and Ian catch each other's eye as I put another biscuit in my mouth and my gaze begins to flit between them, silently asking for an explanation for the obvious look I noticed. Ian scratches his arm absently as he answers my look. "We were more thinking of McEwan house gardens."

It takes me a second to place why going there deserves a look, it's a much nicer area, part of the grounds of an old estate I think, but got changed into public gardens years ago. Then the beginning of it dawns on me, the gardens are really near my house. I cut my eyes over to Ivy and she doesn't even blink.

"We thought we could pick up Katie on the way."

There it is. I'm not really surprised or annoyed, except for them trying to keep it a little hidden from me. As I swallow down the last biscuit in the pack, I mull it over quickly in my head. I might have argued it, said it would tire her out too much or if we were going to see her, we could just stay in, but it's Ian's face that does it, he looks so hopeful at the prospect of me saying yes.

"Fine, we can see." I say, still focussing on his face, which breaks into a grin. Ivy squeals excitedly and bounces off the counter, jumping into my arms, which have to open quickly for there to be anywhere for her to jump into. I catch her, but am glad for the counter right behind me, otherwise we could've ended up a heap on the floor.

Ian starts talking about us grabbing food on the way over but Ivy flaps her hand to cut him off, saying she's got it sorted, making me sure our party is going to grow in number for this picnic. He shrugs and accepts it, Ian may not know about the nature of Ivy or my new friends but he seems to have accepted that they're capable of a lot. He's probably putting it down to them having a lot of money or something, that's the only kind of magic people normally believe in.

CHAPTER 28

We just manage to catch the bus to my house, Ivy says that she doesn't like to drive and that it's just Danny's car they use normally. I try to decipher whether this is true, normally they don't seem to divide ownership of anything, and she could just be saying it like they do to appear more human, but I decide it doesn't matter.

While we take our seats, Ivy's thumbs are flying over her phone as she "makes plans" so me and Ian leave her to it. Filling the time complaining about classes and tutors and everything there is to complain about when it comes to university, which is everything. Occasionally Ivy lifts her head to smile at a particularly whiney comment of ours or to give us an update on plans. My eyebrows raise when she mentions balloons, but there seems to be no question about them being there, only a question of which colour we should get. Me and Ian instantly reply "pink".

Getting off the bus, I'm informed that the others will meet us at the gardens so there's no need to wait. I lead them to the house though they both know full well where it is and begin to worry that we won't be able to take Katie with us. I may be protective of her, but I'm still nothing when it comes to my mum.

"Hey guys." I call as I unlock the door, unsure who is in but hoping someone is.

My mum's head instantly pops into view from the living room. "I am not a guy, Will." She says, eyes sharp before she hugs me. "And who is this?" She says her voice suddenly filled with delight, so I know she's not talking about Ian.

Stepping away from her and turning, I take in Ivy as my mum is seeing her, a girl I'm bringing round to meet her. I'm convinced she's ignoring Ian's presence in this situation. I try not to let my groan escape my lips. "This is Ivy, a *friend* of Ian's and mine from school."

Ian's head tilts in confusion at the 'from school' and my mum's head tilts in sadness at the 'friend', all while Ivy continues to grin, before she bounces forward and gives my mum a far gentler tackle of a hug than she gave me. "It's nice to meet you Mrs. Murphy."

My mum is flustered as Ivy releases her and looks on the verge of pinching Ivy's cheek for her cuteness. "And nice to meet you, dear."

I try to take advantage of my mum's moment of joy at finding a friendly teenager. "We were hoping to take Katie for some fresh air." I blurt, saying fresh air instead of picnic is a better tactic.

My mum's eyes take a moment to leave Ivy and I wonder if she's being quite literally charmed by her. "Hmm." Her eyes clear as they meet mine and I see worry settle into them, my mum likes routine, especially for Katie and I'm threatening to ruin it for the day.

But Ivy steps in before my mum's mouth is able to form the 'no' in her eyes. She places her hand on my mum's arm and catches her gaze again. "We wouldn't take her out for very long and you could have a lie down." Her voice is soft and empathetic, almost a mimic of Lily's, and I see my mum melt a little into her soothing tones.

"I am quite tired." Her head turns back to me and a sleepy smile plays across her lips. "Ok, that's fine Will, but keep an eye on her." My mum makes a start for the stairs and her hand slides over my arm as she does so. When she reaches my level, I notice the stark darkness of the circles under her eyes and am glad Ivy soothed her into sleeping, she probably needs to crash more than I do.

Turning to grin at both Ian and Ivy, I follow my mum up the stairs, sure I'll find Katie in her room. As I reach the landing and push myself through her door, I lower myself down so my head pops through at the normal height of my waist. "Hey Kit Kat."

My beautiful sister is sitting on her bed, Winston the dog in one hand and a giant ladybird toy in the other, from the way she's holding them I'm sure I've interrupted yet another marriage ceremony between soft toys. Proving me right, Katie gives a harsh shush to me before she returns her attention to the animals and announces, "I do." Before shoving their heads, rather harshly, together.

I grin and bring myself back up to my full height and walk over to her bed, I lean my head down to level with hers and repeat, "Hey Kit Kat."

Her bright face turns towards mine and she laughs at my close proximity. "Are we taking a break?"

I laugh to myself, happy she's giving me a good lead in, and scoop her up into my arms, making her squeal. I lower her back down slightly and make intense eye contact with her, my voice a sharp whisper. "Shhh, we're staging a prison break. Picnic, balloons, you name it and no mums allowed." Part of me feels bad for the mum comment, but honestly, that will be half the fun for Katie, she needs some parent free time.

Her eyes grow ever wider as she takes in my serious face, and she realises I mean business, and her little voice responds, "Let's go."

As I sweep her out the room, bundled under one arm, I use the other to grab the travel oxygen tank lying by the door, she hates using it, but if she has as much fun as it looks like she's planning on, she's going to need it.

Half way down the stairs Katie notices Ian and Ivy at the bottom and squeals again. "Uncle Ian!"

Ian immediately opens up his arms scoops her away from me, mocking tossing her in the air, and Ivy grins at the side lines. I realise that though Ivy has met Katie, in her pretence of being a fairy, Katie does not know they've met.

"Katie, this our director of fun today, Ivy, her and our friends are going to give you the best day ever." I pronounce, putting heavy emphasis on the last four syllables.

Katie takes just one look at Ivy before turning away from her slightly bouncing figure and looking at me over Ian's arm around her. She asks in a dramatically hushed tone, "Is she a pixie?"

I laugh as her words remind me, that when describing pixie's, I'd had Ivy as inspiration, though admittedly I had described another face of hers. Leaning in close to her ear I tell her, "Yes." And watch as the whole day ahead of us, instantly becomes magic.

Ian takes over talking to Katie, telling her about all the fun we're going to have, allowing me, I know, to go round the house and grab everything we need for a day out with Katie, half of which she would scorn me for taking along. I shove everything into a large flowery shoulder bag of my mum's and notice Ivy beside me just as I toss it over my right shoulder.

"I didn't like interrupting them." She explains as I catch her eye. I look behind her and see Ian and Katie talking as he swings her from side to side. From the look on their faces I think Ian may be telling Katie about the fact he likes Ivy, he shares his secrets and feelings with her as much as I do, Katie is like a safe.

"Shall we go?" I ask, raising my voice, to give them a moment to bring themselves out of their conversation.

Everyone around me nods vigorously and I begin ushering us out the door, running through my mental check list of stuff to bring as I do.

The gardens are right around the corner from my house, at times in my childhood it seemed to mock my parents, as easy access to fun outdoor activity to keep us healthy, which we never took full advantage of. For the whole short walk round, Katie barely takes a breath as she rattles off stories of the past few days, funny things mum and dad have said, she tells us about the stories they've read her as though they were things that really happened, and, of course, she tells us all about the pretty fairy that lives in our garden, luckily she's looking at Ian for that story.

You access the gardens via an elaborate iron gate that stretches right over my head, the twisted metal scribbles out a cursive 'McEwan' at the top, I think the gate is a remnant of when the grounds were private. We cross through the gate and Katie stretches herself back, still in Ian's arms to read the letters at the top, as she settles herself back down her eyes pop, as she catches sight of the burst of colour ahead of us.

There are two large bundles of brightly coloured helium balloons, along with an assortment of other balloons lying around the large picnic blanket covered in food that our party stands around. Cara and Lily stand next to each other in pretty summer dresses, with Danny and Sam looking deep in conversation in casual clothes on the opposite side to them, Danny though casual is still in dark clothes. I see Ella partially hidden behind one bundle of balloons, kneeling down rearranging the food around her, she too wears a summer dress, in pale blue.

Katie begins clapping, guessing, correctly, that this is her party. Ian jogs over to the others while Ivy runs full out towards them, I follow, lugging the heavy bag on my shoulder. Upon reaching the blanket, Ian places Katie down onto it and kisses her head before standing to clasp Sam's hand in greeting. I notice with a small pleasure that he doesn't do the same to Danny. Dropping my bag as I reach them, I extend an assortment of greetings to everyone, a hug to Lily and Sam, a nod to Danny and a wave to Cara and Ella.

Without taking a breath to allow herself to settle into the group around her, Katie immediately continues with her story telling, this time talking directly to Ella, who smiles fondly at her and nods along. I watch the two talk, slightly from a distance, but am distracted by Lily handing me a cupcake, I take it and grin at the rainbow of sprinkles dotted over it, she leans up to me and says in my ear, out of Ian's earshot. "They're not real, they won't make her sick."

A warmth rises in my chest as I look at Lily and without a word I duck down next to Katie and offer her the pretty lump of sugar. Katie doesn't even stop talking, she grabs it off me and takes a lick of icing in between sentences. I know it's for show, usually the smell of sugar turns her stomach these days, but she knows she loves it, it's the sick inside her that doesn't, and Katie always stays Katie.

Normally, she'll take a lick or a small bite of something and then just keep it in her hand until my mum or I take it from her. As she keeps talking, I see behind her bright eyes the spark of realisation that the frosting actually tastes good to her this time. Next time there's a break in her story she takes a bite, still small, but half icing, half cake. I almost cry when she doesn't spit it out.

Without Katie speaking, she's wholly concentrated on her food now, our group seems oddly quiet, she was making half the noise herself. Everyone else is in little groups having muttered conversations. As the quiet continues my eyes are drawn to Sam, who of course knows how to be the loudest thing with no noise. He's holding up a vivid green frisbee and shaking it to draw everyone else's attention.

"Girls v boys, Katie referees." Ivy immediately announces, beginning to skip a small way away to a clear area of grass. The others, bar me, Ian and Katie follow after her.

Ian calls after them before he moves. "Referees what?"

Cara rolls her eyes prettily. "Frisbee." The 'duh' in her tone is obvious.

Strangely it's Danny who offers us an explanation. "We play it like piggy in the middle, in groups. When you steal possession, you get a point. If the frisbee gets dropped it's first come first serve."

Sounds easy enough, I kiss Katie on the cheek before I get up and jog over, I hear Ian's feet following after me. We all stand there for a second waiting to start and I notice Sam is looking over at my little sister, his eyes asking her to kick things off. Katie is still working on finishing off her cupcake but grins over at us and yells dramatically. "Three…two… one…Throw!"

Sam throws to Danny, who has to catch it like an American football to avoid a tackle from Ivy, who apparently means business, ducking around her he tosses to Ian. As Ian throws to me, I see a dancing flame of red fabric coming towards me and have to snatch it away from Cara, she attempts to do a block of me but has trouble taking herself seriously and collapses, sniggering into her hands, I toss the frisbee over her head to Danny. He's the furthest from me but there had been a straight path to him, he runs forward but Lily floats in and grabs the frisbee from above her own head.

"One to the girls." Shouts Katie, excitedly. From her tone I can tell she's going to be siding with the girls in her cheering.

Lily grins and makes a throw to Ivy who fumbles her catch and drops the disk. Her and Sam make a dive for it and wrestle on the ground, her laughing, him grinning, while the rest of us cheer our teammates on.

The rest of the game passes in a blur of more drops, several tackles, a couple clothes getting severe grass stains and finishes with Ella yanking the frisbee out from right under my nose and then dropping it in surprise that she managed to do so. As we all walk back to Katie, she's still cheering for the girls, who lost points-wise, but still seem to be winners in her eyes. Cara flounces down onto the blanket and reaches for a can of lemonade, before decanting it into a glass, unable to lower herself into drinking straight from it.

Everyone else is bearing witness to Katie's retelling of the game we just played. In her version she doesn't use names except for me and Ian, possibly because we never did introductions with her and the others, but instead describes everyone as a colour. The girls in the colour of their dresses; Cara red, Lily white, Ella blue; with Ivy described as a rainbow; the boys in the colour of their tops; Danny black and Sam green. Her story makes me think of the game as me and Ian playing with balls of different coloured moving light or energy, which is possibly, accidentally, most apt of Katie.

Looking away from her, I catch Cara looking down at her crumpled, lightly stained dress with disgust. I lean closer to her, "Why don't you change?" Her bright eyes flash at me, so I continue, "I know Ian and Katie couldn't see it can't you do it just for some people? Help you feel a bit better." I personally don't care how Cara looks but I know this disgruntled look is killing her.

"I can but it gives me a headache." She answers, grumbling at having to admit a weakness.

I shrug back at her and leave Cara to glaring at her dress. Turning back to the others conversation I see Lily pulling a little dress out of a bag at her feet and holding it up in front of her. It's made of a couple layers of thin white fabric, held by small straps at the top and ending in a different uneven hem at each layer, the top and bottom of the dress are dotted with sewn on multi-coloured buttons of varying sizes. The dress is tiny, and I see that Lily is holding it out to Katie who is reaching for it with her tiny hands, mouth open in awe. "Do you want to try it on?" Lily suggests, her voice gentle, allowing any answer.

Katie doesn't take her eyes off the dress as she bobs her head up and down. Lily ducks down to let her do just that, and gives me a look at the same time, giving me a moment to stop her. Which I don't. I watch as Ella helps Katie off with her shirt, so Lily can slip the dress over her head before they both help Katie shimmy out of the trousers she wears. As she stands up in her dress and twists herself around to watch the skirts of the dress flair out around her, her face is shining so brightly I almost need to look away, but I can't, and never want to.

After taking the dress in herself, Katie looks up at all of us gathered around us, "What do you think?" Her little voice asks. A small wave of compliments from all of us wash over her, like when the tide is moving in and the rush of water fizzes over your feet.

I watch as Ella leans forward on her knees and places a delicate hand on one of Katie's cheeks, her fingers brushing the pink and purple scarf at Katie's head and softly says, "I think you would look even prettier without this." Slowly Ella begins to shift the scarf off of Katie and I see Katie's eyes shimmering as she does so, but as the fabric slides off, I notice a little sigh escape Katie's chest. We are all held for a moment, frozen in place watching Katie and Ella look at each other, before Ella smiles and whispers, as though just for Katie's ears. "Beautiful."

CHAPTER 29

We only start to pack up the picnic when I notice the time, we've been gone four hours and I'm sure the 'spell' Ivy put my mum in won't last forever. If she wakes up with Katie not home, she'll be panicked. The clean-up doesn't take that long, I pack up my stuff while Sam packs up the rest, and everyone else passes the time by bursting the balloons around our feet and taking turns on the helium. Ian has half our group in hysterics with over the top impression of being a killjoy, i.e. me, when it's his turn, Ivy actually falls over while clutching at her stomach, howling.

Just as Sam and I hike the bags onto our shoulders and we're getting set to depart, Katie sneaks up on tiptoe, cartoon-style, behind Danny and makes a grab for his hand. He whips around to see what she'd doing but is too late, she steps away giggling as he sees the sweetie bracelet she's slid onto his wrist. As he holds up his hand, the pastel coloured beads of sugar make a stark contrast to his black ensemble and half of me expects him to rip off the gesture. Instead he smiles tightly and begins walking away, bracelet still in place. Cara gives Katie a high five.

We walk slowly as we leave the gardens, the fastest of us only moving at an amble. Katie is between Ian and Ella, her hands in theirs as she not so subtly suggests they swing her in the air; Sam and Lily walk arm in arm with Cara and Ivy just behind them already bickering about something, though I can just about make out notes of affection in their voices. I end up at the back of the group walking side by side with

Danny, wondering which of us is more annoyed by this, knowing it is probably him.

I really try to let the walk pass with us in absolute silence but when a question pops into my head it finds its way out of my mouth before I can slam it down. "Why do you wear so much black?"

The look Danny gives me makes me regret asking immediately, but I've started, so I just grab a shovel and start digging myself into the conversation. "I mean you don't really strike me as an emo, so is it a stylish thing or...?" I trail off as his dark eyes burn through my skull, and turn towards the people walking ahead of us.

Danny's eyes are still trained on me and I dart my own around to try and distract myself but land on looking at the way Lily and Sam's arms are linked. It's so proper, the distance they keep from each other, the locked way Sam holds his elbow at the perfect angle, it looks copy and pasted out of a period drama. I close my eyes as another thought comes to mind, and I truly try to resist saying it but, "Is it a mourning thing? You know, like traditional wearing of black?"

My eyes stay closed while I walk, waiting for Danny to punch me or shout at me for asking him a personal question, and I silently pray that I'm wrong and he just really likes black. The silence continues between us and I find myself sneaking a glance over at him before immediately stopping, his eyes are like the eye of a storm of dark emotions and I can't bring to look into them for fear of getting trapped in the whirlwind.

Danny lets out a long low breath before he starts talking, and his pace slows to a crawl, some invisible force slowing me down with it. "They mentioned it the first time you met us. Do you remember?"

I rummage through my memories of that day, ransack the piles of information and sensory overload from my first proper time in that house, with these people, then I find it. "There used to be another one, of you." I say it in a hushed tone, it doesn't feel like the kind of thing that should be said brazenly.

His head nods slowly, he stops walking, the rest of our group is almost at my house now, they're going to have to wait apparently. "He was Adam." Danny begins, speaking as though trying to keep his voice steady. "He was with Ella, always. She didn't actually used to be called Ella, she was called Eve. They took those names after Cara made a comment about them being together from the start. She only became Ella...after.

"Adam got restless, he found being human boring, the culture and advancement, it was too slow for him. He missed being what we started out as, he got caught up in the idea of going back but having the kind of consciousness we do now. We all tried to talk him out of it, we don't understand how we became *this*. We couldn't be sure he could find his way back.

"Him and Ella argued for years about it. Decades really. They couldn't understand why the other didn't just back down. I tried to talk to him too, but he was obsessed, the further we tried to push him from the idea of going back, the harder he pushed against us.

"He didn't tell us before he did it. He left a note and vanished. When we were, like we were before, we didn't have any physical existence, we couldn't find each other like that, we don't even know if it worked.

"We know loss, we've all lost every kind of love time and time again, we know how to get back up after it, but those times of grief, they have a body, they have proof of death of the person we loved being over, gone. With Adam, we had no body, and he might not have really been gone. We lived a decade waiting for him to pop back to us, appear in front of Ella and hold her again, after that long, we couldn't keep expecting him to just come back. For the next few years Ella screamed.

"She screamed and cried for years, until she stopped. Then she stood up and kept going, but not really. She stayed in the house, with us and ignored the rest of the world. If she went outside, she knew she'd be looking at every face, looking for him, imagining she saw him. She couldn't do that to herself, until you."

CHAPTER 30

Danny's voice had sounded like extracting poison from an old wound, he didn't get it all out but enough that I knew the pain of it. I'd been staring at Danny frozen in place by his story, surprised and horrified as it went on, but the last two words stopped me short. My head reels as I continue to stare, but the open look on Danny's face makes me realise another reason he hates me so much.

"You're protective of her." I say, no question in my mind. If he continued to wear black at least over a decade after the loss of Adam, they must have been something to each other. The way he'd spoken Adam's name had reminded me of the way I would talk about Ian, with a familiarity bordering on brotherhood. If Ella had been with Adam for nearly the amount of time it sounded like they had been, that must have formed a bond between Ella and Danny, so must the loss have done.

He nods, though I don't need it, and glances over at the others, who are indeed waiting for us, arranged haphazardly around the wall and gate leading to my front door. Before he moves to reach them, he says, finality in his voice. "You hurt her, and I'll break you."

A shiver erupts down my spine before I can continue moving as well, no doubt he means that, but along with the shiver there is a flurry in my stomach as another meaning of his words comes to mind. For there to be even the chance of me hurting her, which I would never do, there has to be even the slimmest possibility of something happening between us. I try not to skip to my house.

Reaching my door, I'm not sure if everyone is expecting to be invited in, but I hear Lily begin to say goodbye to Katie and turn to see the others bundled around her ready to do the same. Ian stands apart from them, smiling at me. Katie hugs them all in turn, jabbering about all the fun she has had. I walk back towards them to gather Katie up in my arms, knowing that despite the fact she has just been sitting the whole time in the garden, and the food she'd had, she hadn't really had, the excitement will have been draining. She fusses a little as I pick her up, but it's mostly since she thinks I'll ruin her new dress. I add my goodbyes to hers as the group moves to leave, and find it difficult to take my eyes away from Ella, who is beaming at me, her brown hair twisting around her face in the breeze, if I wasn't holding Katie, I could have brushed it away.

Ian claps my shoulder as he takes the bag from it and pushes ahead through my front door and Katie wraps her arms around my neck settling against my chest. In the house, I notice the quiet, straight away, my mum must still be asleep, and I guess my dad is out. Ian is in the living room rifling through the shelves next to the tv, suggesting different games we could play, assuring us he is gifted at snakes and ladders, but against my chest I feel Katie yawn into me and nudge my head towards her, eyes wide at Ian, pointing it out.

"You know what Katie? Me and Will should read you a story. I swear I do the best voices." He says, tugging himself upright, getting what I mean straight away.

"Yeah right." I laugh in response. "I do the best voices, bar none."

Katie giggles sleepily and turns her head to eye us both. "I'll referee." She says.

We all laugh and Ian climbs after me as I take Katie upstairs. While we're going through her mini bookshelf debating what to read, Katie's soft breathing gives us pause, turning we see she's already asleep in her bed where I placed her, Winston snuggled into her, one floppy ear over her face.

The sofa downstairs feels more comfortable than I ever remember it being when I crash into it, I hadn't realised how worn out I was again. Ian kicks my legs off the far end of the sofa and crashes into the other side, leaning his head right back against the rest, obviously feeling the same as I do. It's a moment before we recover enough from the joy of sitting down, to speak.

"How are you feeling about Ivy?" I ask him, wanting to be a good friend and check in.

Ian raises his head back to a normal position and slowly nods as he says, "She's a good friend."

Knowing he needs to just talk about her like that, in friend terms, in order to stop thinking about her in more than friend terms, I nod along with him. "A really good friend."

"You and that Danny guy seemed to be having a heart to heart." From Ian's tone I know he's prying, and remember his comment about me not sharing that much. I do want to work on that, but there's only so much I can share about the others.

"He was giving me a big brother-esque speech about not hurting Ella. She had a lot of drama with an ex." That is simplifying things to an extreme, but it covers the gist.

Ian continues nodding, and as we sit in our low positions on the sofa and have the beginnings of a probable big, deep conversation, I have the odd feeling we should both have beer cans in our hands. It's unlikely my parents have any in, and even less likely they'd be ok with me having some, the fact I'm overage is yet to hit them.

"He scared you off?" Asks Ian, his eyebrow raising at me, and a quirk in his growing smile.

Ella's face comes forth in my mind, her laughing at Ian, looking bewildered during frisbee, and smiling gently at Katie. "No chance."

"Didn't think so." Says Ian, the smile he gives me is so contagious, that I offer one right back.

As we continue to look at each other his smile fades to seriousness. "Thank you, for today. For letting us all be there."

The fact he feels gratitude for me allowing a day like today makes me squirm in my seat, the day had been so full of colour and fun for everyone, I found it hard to remember why I normally kept people away. Of course, as I think I remember that without the others being there, the weather would've been miserable, Katie wouldn't have even been able to stomach the smell of the food around her and we wouldn't have been able to conjure that beautiful dress that would be a memento of a day so alive for her. I was starting to believe that they truly could help Katie, well in a smaller way than I'd wanted them to originally, which I appreciate but still feel a sting looking into Ian's face, that him and I aren't capable of the same.

I'd been staring at Ian's face while those words spun through my mind, and just as the revelations from Danny begin joining them Ian brings me back by bursting out laughing. "It was just a thank you, no need to freak out dude." The second 'dude' in one day, strange, but I laugh back anyway.

It's another two hours before my mum emerges from her room, her hair tousled into a soft cloud and a still sleepy smile on her face. Ian and I are still sprawled on the sofa but have placed a game of snakes and ladders between us, it's juvenile, but Ian truly has a gift for missing the snakes. We quickly inform my mum that Katie is asleep and has been fine all day, I'd snuck up after my first lost game to place the oxygen around her wee ears and nose, knowing she'll feel better for it when she wakes up.

My mum simply nods and joins us, placing herself on the floor between us and picking up a red counter to join our game.

CHAPTER 31

The next couple of days pass in a blur of me actually catching up on both uni work and sleep. The others have ignored the plan we laid out and are, in some form or another, all doing something every day to cheer Katie up or give some inspiration for a tale she can later tell me on the phone when I call. Ivy has even gone to the house a couple times to offer babysitting services for my mum to get more sleep too, she is quickly so well rested that my dad is slightly panicked by it.

When I say my mum is well rested, I am being generous. For the past year she's been on the verge of insomnia, and often wakes up multiple times in the night, her mind abuzz. Ivy stepping in has giving my mum the opportunity to nap, in place of pounding caffeine.

Ian and Jack also come to me at the start of the week with assurances they are falling behind in their classes and that we all need a library study group together, a scheme, I'm sure, to force me into the library and onto my work. I doubt Jack knows that this a scheme to help me out, he really is behind on his classes, and is benefitting more than I am, but he is also not being dragged there by the arm, like I am by Ian.

Isaac hasn't made any mention of him having to literally lead me to bed the other night and lull me to sleep. Instead he knocks on my door most nights and offers to make me a hot chocolate. I only take him up on the offer one night, and we spend the time drinking the molten brown goodness, catching up on our relationship lives, he is very excited about the prospect of me and a girl. Overall, I am becoming more sure surer, that anyone Isaac dates needs to be an angel to be worthy of him, which his guy apparently is.

I'm just reading a long paragraph Lily sent me, telling me that Katie is currently trying to read Sam's mind telepathically, when I type back the small message I've been debating sending to her or one of the other girls since they started sending me updates. "Can you send me Ella's number?" My heart pounds erratically as I press send. Only Lily, Cara and Ivy have been texting me, Lily is always with Sam and I assume his muteness stands for messaging. Danny has not visited though he is apparently responsible for the basket of candy bracelets on Katie's bedside table. Ella has visited but there have been not texts accompanying them.

"Ella doesn't have a phone." Comes Lily's quick reply. I exhale. I didn't think any of them really *had* phones, they're just one of the things they have when they need them. Maybe Ella refuses to ever have one, my aunt is like that, she refuses to have a phone and when her bank made it necessary for online banking, she shut down her account instead of getting one. Technophobia could be applicable to Gods too.

I don't know what else to say so just shove my phone back in my pocket, I'm going to my house later on but am under strict orders, from both my dad and Cara, an unlikely pairing, that I cannot head round until I've at least made a start on my final essay of the semester for English. So far, only the title stretches across my word document, which I doubt they'll think is enough. I'm always alright once I start essays, but getting myself to start is the challenge.

The buzzer for our flat rings and my fingers flinch on the keyboard I am poised at, causing utter gibberish to spill onto the page. Without pausing to delete it, I bound out of my chair to get the door, making a bet on who it's for. I do this every time I answer the door when not expecting anyone, and always guess Isaac, it means I've never been wrong, but today I feel bad, so bet on Eric. I am wrong, but not for the reason I think.

Ella is standing in my doorway, smiling shyly. She's lugging two massive bags which I reach forward to take, to hide my utter shock, and awe.

"Thank you." She says, using her now free hand to rearrange her jacket which has gone mightily askew. She's wearing a Tartan, kilt-style, skirt with a thin blue jumper, paired with riding boots and a denim jacket. She looks amazing, and I glance down at the bags I've taken for something to do.

"What's this?" I ask dumbly. I'm looking down at obvious groceries; bread, milk, eggs, cheese, pasta, fruit, veg, biscuits and crackers.

Ella coughs awkwardly before speaking. "Ivy said your kitchen was pretty bare so I thought I'd bring stuff round." Her blue eyes reach into my green ones. "Is that okay?"

I almost laugh but don't want it to look like I'm laughing at her, so settle for smiling broadly. "Of course. Oh come in." I add, realising I'm blocking her entry.

Still looking nervous, Ella does a little hop passed me in the hallway and wanders down it, head whirring around at every detail. I follow after her, trying to work out how to react to this all normally, I have never wanted a wing man so much, or just another person in the room. If Ivy was here, I could tell from the way she buzzed around what she wanted me to do.

There's a little window in the door leading into our kitchen/living space, so Ella knows which door to go through and pushes into it, holding the door open for me. I give her a nod of thanks, these bags are frighteningly heavy.

In silence, I start to unpack the bags, trying to think of something, anything to say. I should probably thank her for the food but the words can't seem to find their way out my mouth. Ella is looking around as though for a stool to perch on, but we don't have any, the options are the overly squishy sofa at the far end of the room, or balancing on the counter. Ella goes for neither and instead moves forward to help me unpack.

"Thank you." I say, weakly.

Ella just smiles.

I pause as I put the milk into fridge, reading the sell by date, a thought occurring to me.

"I actually bought it. It's all got lasting nutritional effects." Ella says with a faint chuckle in her tone, correctly translating the look on my face.

"Ah good." I say, dropping the milk into the shelf. "Another thought springs to mind. "Was this your first time in a shop?"

Ella grins, it's small but it's there. "Yes. It was quite fun." The excitement in her voice reminds me of Ivy about everything.

Laughing I say. "That's great. You should make a list of all the new things you've got to try." I don't think before I say it, and suddenly worry that it's the wrong thing to say, she's not spent any time outside in years, is it pushy to mention doing it more? A lot more? Or is it just a stupid thing to say generally?

"Like rollercoasters?" Says Ella, her voice a cocktail of excitement, with nerves shaken in.

"Yeah, or uh, modern art galleries." I say, trying to sound cultured.

Ella's eyes widen and we continue to list all the new things in the world for the last few decades, which admittedly is a lot. After we finish unpacking food, we start doing the dishes, and drying them together, just to have something to do with our hands, other than have them hang limply at our sides.

Isaac bustles into the room in a whirlwind, as usual, and starts talking as soon as he sees me. Not noticing Ella who is now rearranging fridge magnets while I wipe the counters. "Wow, our kitchen has never been tidier, and I'm about to mess it up again." Says Isaac, voice full of mirth as he rubs his hands together before tearing open the cupboard and scooping supplies out. "I only have like 5 minutes before I have to be off, seeing a film with my guy and he's a weirdo who hates to miss the trailers."

Ella gasps from the behind us. "Oh, the cinema, I forgot about that. New films must be so interesting."

Isaac whirs around, loaf of bread in hand, as soon as Ella makes a noise. The shock in his face makes me realise this is possibly the first time he's seen a girl in our flat; he's friends with guys and has never brought a girl round, I only have Ian round occasionally and Isaac missed Ivy being here, and Eric has never brought anyone to the flat as far as we know.

As his face continues not to move while staring at her, Ella's nerves come back, almost visibly, as pink rises in her cheeks. Isaac finally gets over himself and reaches out a hand that's not preoccupied with bread. "Sorry, hi I'm Isaac."

Ella's hand shakes ever so slightly as she raises it up to his. "Nice to meet you, I'm Ella." Her voice is tight and prim from nerves but Isaac doesn't notice. A grin blossoms over his face as she says her name, I've told him Ella is the girl we've recently been talking about.

"Oh, Ella, would you like to join us at the cinema? Will could come to." His tone matches hers in an unconscious attempt to put her at ease, Isaac likes to put everyone at ease. It's also the most obvious kind of set up he's doing here, inviting me and the girl I like along to a date with his boyfriend. Luckily, Ella is out of date with her social cue knowledge and doesn't seem to notice.

"That sounds lovely!" Her voice trills with excitement and I can't help but laugh at her enthusiasm.

"It's a double date then." says Isaac, dropping her hand and returning the bread quickly back to its cupboard and slamming the door shut again in a heartbeat. Turning back to us, his face drops slightly at the shock on both our faces, Ella's because of what he just said and mine, because he admitted that was his goal. "We can keep air quotes round the word -date- if you want." He says, making the first two fingers of each hand bounce like bunny ears.

Just then his phone rings and he ducks into the hall to answer it after making a quick, one minute, signal. His boy-friend, along with liking to see the trailers also likes to talk on the phone rather than text or message.

I can't bring myself to look at Ella, but she breaks the growing silence before I have to. "He reminds me of Ivy." The sound of her voice is all warmth as she says it.

I think about her words before I respond, and smile at the thought, I see Ella's point, both Isaac and Ivy move around the world in a bounce and a fizz of movement, I imagine watching their conversation and having to move your head between them so fast it's like you're watching an Olympic level ping pong game. "I see that." I agree, my voice with matching warmth.

We catch each other's eye and the warmth seems to fizzle out through the whole kitchen. Isaac pops his head back through the door and the bubble bursts.

"You guys coming?"

Seeing Ella nod, I bob past Isaac to grab my jacket from my room. I pause for a second when I pick it up and look outside my room's window, the sky is a white plain of cloud, and I can see trees being blown about in the wind. I grab a scarf from the back of my door as I leave again.

Isaac and Ella are laughing about something when I re-enter the kitchen, which causes a small rush of paranoia up my chest but I push it down and hold the scarf out for Ella, it's made of soft, blue, knit wool. "It looks pretty cold out." I say in explanation. As the words leave my mouth, I become aware that Ella probably doesn't feel the cold and feel instantly stupid.

She takes the scarf anyway, and with a whispered word of thanks begins to wind the long thin fabric round her neck, I see as she looks back up at me, pulling her hair free, that the blue matches her bright eyes. Looking away from her before I do or say something else stupid, I catch sight of Isaac making heart eyes between us, and try to hurt him with a look. It does not work.

"Let's go!" He says, gesturing us out the door with his arm like Dora the Explorer.

The walk to the cinema isn't far, but we're apparently running late so Isaac insists on us getting the bus. While we wait at the stop, I notice Ella reading the sign for tourists explaining how to pay for your ticket. I reach out my hand and tug at the bottom of her denim jacket to grab her attention, she looks down at where I sit on the edge of the stop's bench. "I'll get your ticket, just get on after me."

She smiles gratefully and sits down on the bench too, bouncing her knee in anticipation. I grin at my lap. Isaac ignores us both, since he's back to talking on the phone with his boyfriend, smiling widely himself. Gosh, we must look like idiots, there's only a little old lady at the stop apart from us and she keeps giving us a half glower, for looking so happy to be getting the bus. She probably thinks we should be walking, what with our youthful energy and uncracking joints.

Ian, Felix and I used to get annoyed when old people gave us looks for getting on the bus for short journeys. There was a couple of weeks when one of us would fake a terrible limp whenever we caught someone glaring at us, to make them feel bad for judging. I both hold back a laugh and grimace at the memory now, but as we see our bus approaching and stand up for it, I have the urge to fake a limp, which is difficult to supress.

Isaac bounds on the bus after the woman and Ella shuffles on right after me, so close I'm sure she feels the need to make it perfectly clear to the driver that it's her I'm paying for. I do a little gesture to her before I put the money in the machine to put her at ease. We follow Isaac up the stairs on the bus, despite the fact we won't be on it long enough for it to be worth going upstairs. He's stretched out over one side of the seats upfront and I go for the one by the window on the opposite side, Ella sits between us, looking cutely unsure.

Trying to put her at ease again, I just start talking. "When I used to get the bus with Katie, she always wanted to sit up here, we'd pretend to drive, even though we had no idea what we were doing, we just shouted 'break' and 'indicate' every so often with our hands up like they were holding onto a wheel. I still have no clue how to drive, can't be bothered with lessons, my dad took me out once and I think we both count it as a near death experience. My mum doesn't drive either, she cycled when she was a kid and all the times she was cut off by cars and things put her off, she refuses to become a car person." I don't exactly where I'm going with my rambling, but Ella has taken my hand, so I find it hard to care.

CHAPTER 32

The film we all go and see is a sweet animation, definitely meant as a kids' film but we don't care. The main humanoid creature wants to be an artist but can't draw very realistically, my guess is that she's going to create her own art style that's revolutionary, and somehow heart-warming.

As I watch, I'm trying to remember all the main points so I can tell it to Katie as a bedtime story, she can't make it to the cinema very much and hates waiting on things appearing on tv or on DVD. Plus, I like that when I tell the story, I'll be able to make her the artist, though that will probably ensure a drawing phase and force our mum to plaster our fridge door and cupboard fronts even more fully, in a collage of bad drawings. I love Katie, but her drawings are something I find it hard to find enthusiasm for.

Ella had jumped when the adverts had started up, and her head had whipped around the theatre trying to find the source of the surround sound, and her eyes had grown into the size of the frisbee we'd played with the other day as the screen had illuminated to show an overly complicated whir of colours that somehow promoted buying a car. I'd laughed silently and nudged her arm to bring her back into reality, she'd looked close to falling right into the screen.

Now she is fully enraptured by the film, smiling along, but only laughing at about half the jokes, a lot go over her head as references. There are a few things Ella laughs at where she is the only one, things we all recognise as old boring tropes of films, are new to her.

Our group are sharing a very odd kind of snack. Isaac's boyfriend had arrived before us and bought a huge box of mixed popcorn, and eaten through the top layer of it. Isaac had brought his own snacks, with his pockets crammed with all kinds of sugary sweets. When we'd taken our seats in the cinema, Isaac had snatched the popcorn from his boyfriend and emptied all his sweets into the top of the box before carefully shaking the box around to try and mix everything up. While he was doing so, Ella and Isaac's boyfriend, who I think is called Charlie, but Isaac refers to him by name so little that I'm not entirely sure, anyway both his and Ella's faces were a mixture of intrigue and disgust, while I am too used to watching Isaac cook to be surprised. In the end it tastes pretty good mixed together, and whenever I'm handed the box, Ella will reach out for a timid handful and chew each bit slowly.

The film ends in the way I predict, and the heart-warming moment at the end gets to me and Charlie, who I catch rubbing his eye as the credits start. Isaac stands as soon as the film is over and starts putting on his jacket, but flops back down as he sees that none of the rest of us are moving.

Katie always watches the credits of films until she sees her first name pass over the rolling names and job titles on screen. So it's only after I see an 'Assistant Costume Designer #3: Katie McGowan' that I move to put my own jacket back on. When I start to move, Ella follows after me, joining in Isaac and his boyfriend's discussion about the film.

Out of the cinema I turn my phone back on and a text comes through from Ivy, "Ella with you?" I look over at Ella, still talking to the guys before I text back a quick "Yes. We were just at the cinema." In case she sent the text a while ago.

Isaac and Charlie are going to head for some dinner, which Isaac is especially energetic about doing since he didn't make himself anything at the flat earlier. I feel like we've taken up enough of their date time so make zero attempt to join them, and instead turn to Ella.

"Do you want me to walk you home?"

With those words I can almost see it dawn on Ella that she's been out of the house for a long time, possibly the longest in years, without any of the others with her. This makes it dawn on me that the text from Ivy may have had a hint of panic attached.

"Yes, thank you." Says Ella, her eyes brightening again as she brings herself out of her thoughts.

We wave to the guys as they head in the opposite direction to go off and be coupley together, but before they depart, Isaac reaches forward and holds Ella in a brief hug before starting off, I almost think I see him whisper something quick in Ella's ear but brush it off as an imagination.

I check my phone as we walk to see if Ivy has sent anything else but my phone screen remains blank, apart from a junk email notification. "So I guess that's one thing ticked off your list." I say, pushing my phone back in my pocket.

Ella nods, adjusting the scarf I gave her. "We should do more things." Her face pinkens and she quickly stutters, "I mean, I should, that was fun."

I turn my head to face forward to give her a second to get over the embarrassment she feels for that comment and fight doing a little nerdy skip, taking a breath before I say, "I'd like to tick them off with you." Keeping my head forward for my own sake this time.

Ella stops walking, and I do the same, just a few steps ahead of her and turn back, her head is tilted as she looks at me. I don't know what she sees in my face but she says, voice tinged with a chill that I don't think is meant for me. "Danny talked to you." It's not a question.

"Well...yes."

She huffs out a breath making her hair flutter around her head.

"Why does that matter?" I ask.

"I liked you not knowing."

"I like knowing."

There's a beat of silence.

"It doesn't bother you?"

"What doesn't bother me?" I check, feeling like I should be aware of what exactly we're talking about.

"You know..." Ella pauses as though reaching for the word, "I have...baggage."

I laugh, well guffaw really, and try and smother it quickly, seeing her stricken face. "Everyone has baggage." Admittedly, Ella seems to have a lot more pain to lug around that most people, but she's carrying it, that's what matters. Not how long it took her to pick it up.

Another beat of silence passes between us and then Ella starts walking again.

"Could we go to a gallery before a rollercoaster? I think that could be easier to take."

I continue walking as well, and grin, nothing can stop me grinning now. "That's because you've not seen modern art."

We continue talking as we walk home, no more tension in our words, just our new found familiarity. The back of my mind is trying to decide whether we are going on a date when we go to the gallery as we are arranging to do soon, or if we are just meeting up, I decide that people with much more dating experience than me are better placed to work that out.

Arriving back at their house, we find Ivy on the step outside, flicking through a book with her legs crossed. She looks up at our approach and I indeed see a flash of worry, quickly extinguished as she takes us in.

"How was the film?"

Ella wrinkles her nose in a small confusion, before shrugging it off and replying. "It was good, looked weird." The last sentence is said with a slight hesitation.

"They're all weird these days." Says Ivy, lightly. In her orange docs, bell bottom jeans and embroidered vest top, she is the picture of a little weird. She stands up, her book disappearing out her hand as she does so and pushes the door open, eyes questioning whether I am coming in.

"I said I'd drop by my house tonight." I say, uselessly jutting a thumb out in the vague direction of home.

Ivy nods and heads inside, leaving the door cracked open. Ella turns to me, starting to unravel the scarf I'd given her. I really don't want her to give it back. I hold up a hand.

"Keep it, it might be cold when we go to the gallery." Like Isaac inviting her to the cinema, it is obvious what I mean, I want to make sure we do go through with our plans, but again I'm not sure if she will read it like that.

Ella smiles and keeps the scarf around her neck. "Good point." She says, and leans up slowly on her toes before placing a careful chaste kiss on my cheek, time slows as she moves and then speeds up all too fast as she jumps up the step, and into her house.

My mind is a blank haze of happy as I walk to my house, taking each turn on auto pilot.

When I got into the house, Lily and Sam are still there. Sam in the living room with my dad, both silently reading and Lily doing the dishes with my mum, while they chat easily. If my mum had to choose between Lily and Ivy, I don't think she could bring herself to do it. They both wave as I enter and the guys barely look up from their books. Domestic bliss.

I slip upstairs to find Katie asleep in her bed, and press a gentle kiss to her forehead before returning downstairs, and choosing the girls company.

"How was your day?" My mum asks, her eyes clearer than normal as she scrubs at a pot.

"Good, I think I have a date." I say it purely for her reaction and am not disappointed. The pot falls back into the sink with a large, soapy, splash and she squeals like Katie before hugging me. Her gloved hands start soaking the back of my jacket before she lets go.

I laugh. "It's upsetting that you're this surprised."

"I'm not surprised." Supplies Lily, from my mum's side, a knowing smile on her pale face.

My mum splutters. "I'm not, it's not that, can't I be happy for my son?"

I laugh again, and nod at her.

She turns back to her pot, happy for the information but knowing I won't offer her more detail, that would feel too weird.

I stay for just a couple of hours, Sam and Lily are invited to stay for dinner and insist on driving me to my flat afterwards. Lily has prepared a "special" side dish just for Katie, which she assures my mum is healthy and assures Katie, in a whisper, is not, making me sure that in reality the dish is not anything. Katie scoops it up, making everyone happy, but only manages the same amount as usual of her main meal, meaning not very much. My stomach twists as I watch, despite the lighter mood of the meal, nutrition wise, it's the same situation for my sister.

After our meal, I take Katie upstairs and recount the plot of the film to her, and as I had suspected, I have to talk her out of getting her art supplies out right that second. Luckily, I have the story of my day with Ella to settle her down. She'll do anything for gossip.

As I'm heading out the door, my dad slips a couple notes into my jacket pocket, with a murmured comment about my "date", I smile awkwardly at the out dated gesture but don't argue and thank him, before heading out to the car.

CHAPTER 33

By the time Ian and Jack, and everyone else start to worry about exams, I'm starting to feel so separate from them. I doubt I'll be sitting my exams, it's a hard thought to have, because of the reason, but I'm already half preparing to take resits over the summer or something.

Katie, and the rest of my family, are happier and more settled recently, with all the reassurance that the others have been giving us. But I can still see how little Katie is really eating, really standing, really living. Her big eyes are growing more prominent in her face as her whole, little frame, thins. Ian and I are now always careful when we lift and move her, feeling how fragile she is beyond her continuing laughter.

I do go to the gallery with Ella and feel my heart glow at the way she sticks her tongue out at half the exhibitions, and just watch her face as she takes in, silently, one corner of the room that plays out a piece made solely of moving light and shifting projected images. We leave the gallery holding hands.

We still haven't made it to a rollercoaster but we spend a little time together most days, always doing something. Whenever we walk around markets or gardens or museums, Ella allows me to exist in my tangled thoughts for only a few minutes at a time before managing to tug me free of them to take in something new, and removed from our lives.

I started waking up in the night, breathing heavily, worrying away the time before I fall back to sleep, obsessing over the nothing I can do.

Cara invites me to the house to work on our English coursework, and I sit in the library of their house pouring over a couple sources for my last essay, their library is better than Google Scholar.

Danny has been sitting across the expansive room in a stuffed leather armchair, and ignoring us, but he is suddenly next to me and hits the book he holds against my shoulder to knock me out of the train of thought he must've seen me falling into.

I blink up at him, eyeing the book in his hand, whenever he holds a book, I remember all too well our first meeting, when he'd chucked one at my head.

Without a word he gestures for me to follow him and strolls out of the room. I look at Cara before I get up and she silently rolls her eyes at his behaviour. When I'm out of the library, I see that Danny hasn't waited around for me and have to jog a little to catch up with him, he is halfway up the large staircase in the middle of the entrance room that I've never been up. I halt a moment before taking the first step up but then take them two at a time after him.

Reaching the top of the staircase, Danny turns to me, hands in the pockets of his black jeans, a bracelet of sweets still around his wrist. "Ivy showed you that room with all our stuff, right?" It isn't really a question, more him jogging my memory.

I nod. "Briefly." It had been a while ago, while I was still adjusting to them all, I hadn't had the headspace to peruse it, and had actually left pretty quickly. It had been a long hallway adorned with tables upon tables of things across time, the things they held onto.

Danny's head bobs at a pace matching my own. "This is a little like that." Is all he says, before he opens a clean white door near the top of the stairs and walks in.

I follow.

I never know what to expect when I walk into the rooms of this house, so don't bother with expectations and just allow surprise to take hold. My first impression, probably because of all the time I've spent with Ella lately, is that I am in a gallery. We are in a large rectangular room, that fades at the corners, making me suspect that if I walked towards any of them, I would see the walls expand to show more beyond what I see now. The walls are white beneath their decoration but the pieces are so crammed together, it is hard to tell.

Stepping towards the bit of wall closest to me, hardly aware of Danny's eyes on me, I look over the bit of canvas closest to my eye level. It is an unframed oil portrait of a woman, I can make no guess at the exact period of the painting but it is at least a couple centuries old. The woman has rich brown eyes at odds with her done up blonde hair, and her hands are clasped on her lap, holding onto a single red rose.

The piece beneath the first is on what looks like a scrap of parchment, bearing only a simple sketch of a man, his face smiles out from the rough lines and looks as though it may have been sketched during a coffee, or some kind of informal meeting.

The third piece I look at is stuck on the wall, to the side and between the others, a photograph this time, it holds the black and white image of a couple on their wedding day, taken, from the looks of it at the early stage in photo development. It is fuzzy around the edges where each of them have moved. I smile at the image as I notice the faces of the couple are fuzziest, the ghosts of smiles playing around their straight faces, showing they'd had a hard time keeping their faces straight on the happiest day of their lives.

"What are these?" I ask Danny, not turning to face him but roaming my eyes over more of the pieces in front of me, each one holding a new face or faces.

"Our friends. Our families." Answers Danny, his voice too neutral to be believably so.

That makes me turn my head towards him, I point behind my back to the painting of the woman I'd first looked at.

Danny smiles, I try to remember if I've ever seen him smile before. "An old crush of Cara's."

My eyes seek out the painting again and focus on the rose, wondering if it had been given by Cara, if anything had happened, while I am aware with the age of the piece, it is sadly unlikely.

Danny steps forward, and from beside me he points at the bride in the photograph I'd also looked at. "That is Emily, a wonderful dancer."

I smile at the comment and wait for him to say who the man at her side was, when he doesn't I turn to him and see his face looking irritated again, a familiar look on him. "That's me."

"Oh." Is all I can manage, looking again, over the blurred lines of Danny's smile on his wedding day. "Why are you showing me this?" I ask, both trying to move away from this now awkward moment and because I am curious.

"Because I want you to know. That we never forget."

His words hang in the air as I soak them in.

"You won't forget." I say slowly.

He nods. "Never."

The knot that now lives in my stomach loosens, just a little. I've always found the idea of wanting to be famous, silly. Jackie used to talk about wanting to go down in history, and I'd shrugged her off and continued eating my lunch. Now, I think I understand, being remembered, it is something. Not because being famous matters, but there being someone who cares, always, that's something. Danny will always remember Emily, Cara will always remember her crush and I will always remember Katie. So will my mum, my dad and Ian. But 'always' *is* 'always' when Danny and the rest of them say it.

I nod again, not able to really respond, but after a moment I ask, "Can I keep looking around?"

Danny gives a final nod, which is apparently how we communicate, and leaves the room.

I don't know how long I'm in there, but I inch around the room, trying to take in every face, guessing at who knew them, if it was all of them, and trying to spot if any of the faces I look at are Lily's or Ivy's or any of the others from the past.

I'm crouched on the ground looking at another sketched drawing when Cara comes to find me. She coughs pointedly from the doorway and I almost tumble over while turning to face her. "I thought we were studying." She says irritated.

"I was studying, you were copying." I say, sarcastically, getting to my feet ungracefully, before following her out.

As Cara goes to whirl out of the room dramatically, I see her pause as she catches sight of the wall by the door. It must be hard to just walk away from these faces.

"Did you give her the rose?" I just have to ask.

Cara turns back to me, her earlier irritation gone, given way to nostalgia. "I put it in her hair during a dance we went to. Her hair was starting to fall out from all the turning she'd been doing, I put it in to help fasten things together." The smile across her lips is genuine as she speaks and neither of us say another word as we make our way back to the library.

While we continue to work, the smile never quite manages to leave Cara's face.

I'm only out the house by about 5 minutes before I am running back to it to get Danny, or Sam or any of them to drive me.

My dad just called.

CHAPTER 34

It's Sam who drives, he was the first one I found and we were out the door before anyone else could tag along. I hadn't even had to speak, he'd seen my face and begun shoving me out the door immediately, I'd distantly heard the jangle of him picking up the keys on the way.

I appreciate his silence as we drive, my own head too loud to take any more noise. My head is in my hands for half the drive, trying to calm my breath and hold it together until I know more.

My dad had only spoken for a few seconds when I picked up the phone, before one of us had hung up, I don't remember who. Only the key words were important anyway; "Katie", "hospital", "blood". Those three words spiral around my thoughts, picking up speed as time goes on.

Before Sam even stops the car, I am out of it. Sprinting.

There is a queue at reception, but I don't even pause, I continue on, pushing through doors and racing up staircases until I get to the paediatric floor. I almost run straight into Helen, a nurse I recognise as one of the more irritable nurses on the floor.

"Will?!" She says, holding an arm out to stop me, perplexed.

"Where is she?" I ask, demand. Whipping my head around as though I will be able to spot her in a room from the corridor.

"Katie? She's not..." Helen's voice trails off and we stare at each other.

I sprint away again. My heart pounding so hard, my entire body pounding back through the halls I'd come. If Katie is in the hospital but she isn't here, if they haven't seen her, she has to be in the emergency room. It is really an emergency.

Flying through the ER doors, I see everyone and everything else moving at the same pace I am, the wave of action, it doesn't feel calming, but it feels oddly accepting. The way I feel, the burning of my entire body and mind, belongs in a place like this.

Before I even see him, my dad is hugging me. He isn't a hugger, he is a handshaker, a shoulder holder if it's important. I am almost sick right where I stand.

I see a flurry of doctors around a bed, from the glimpses I see, the bed looks empty, or the patient isn't taking up much room on it. I try to move forward, get closer, but my dad's hands grip my chest and arm and won't let me. I turn to him, hurt, and see his eyes are wet.

Shaking my head, I begin backing away but my dad's hands keep me contained, he holds me in place. I don't want to be in place, I have to move, everyone else is moving, doing, I can't not do. Blinking around the space I try to find my mum. "Mum?" I ask the air, breath catching.

"She couldn't. She's outside." My dad gulps a lot as he speaks and he lets go of me, in a motion pushing me gently towards the ambulance entrance.

I move without thinking, or with too much thinking, and find myself outside. My mum is hugging the wall outside, glowering so hard at some smokers a small distance away, she looks as though she may use the wall to propel herself forward in attack.

"Mum?" I say again, voice continuing to break.

She turns to me, it takes her a second, and the glower on her face crumples into something just as dark but founded on sadness, not anger. Looking at it makes me miss the anger.

We collapse into each other and I don't know who's holding who up.

"I can't do this."

I hold her tighter. "You have to." It's true, she has to, we have to. There's no not doing this.

We let each other go just enough to look at each other for a moment, then go back inside.

My dad has found his way into a chair, but every part of him is bouncing and jangling so much in nerves he looks bound to fall out of it. I don't bother attempting to join in the chair next to him, I need to move. I pace.

"Why can't we?" I ask, eyes boring into the door separating us from where the doctors still move in a flurry together, there's at least five of them in there.

They take a moment to answer, my dad begins to move more erratically and my mum is biting her nails, she'll probably draw blood soon. "I threw a pack of swabs at a doctor." My mum finally admits in a rush.

I laugh, the image hilarious to me. I laugh so hard that I double over, clutching at my stomach. I hear my parents join in. We all laugh hysterically, in the centre of the chaos. Then we don't stop. I'm finding it hard to breathe but I just keep laughing, my stomach hurts and my face aches and I still can't stop. My dad has his head in his hands, still shaking and my mum is curled over him, her head resting on his back, her arm around his shoulders.

My laughing finally stops and I collapse from my position onto the floor in front of them.

The room is still full of noise, full of movement so I don't know how we know. But we all turn together as a faint long beep sounds from the room with the doctors, the room with my sister.

We move together and push into the room, and no one stops us. No one could, but they don't even try. They're all shouting, moving even faster than they were before.

I want to move over to her, to hold her hand but I can't see it and I can't move a muscle.

In the rush of doctors, I catch the eyes of one, he must be a medical student, just a child, he's barely older than me. He shouldn't be here for this, I shouldn't be here for this, Katie shouldn't be here for this.

I'm still looking into that student's face when I hear another one of them speak over the others as their movement begins to slow, "Time of..."

My mother screams.

CHAPTER 35

I'm outside. At the ambulance station again and I'm bent over, throwing up. Someone is patting my shoulder. Maybe they're saying something but all I can hear is my mum's scream, it's echoing around every crevice of my brain, taking up all the space. That's all I've got in me now, screaming.

I'm sitting. Still outside, my back against the wall my mum had been leaning against earlier, someone is crouched next to me, I still can't tell if they're talking to me, maybe they're a doctor checking if I'm alright. I'm not. I'm screaming, silently.

I'm looking up at a rainbow. Katie loved rainbows, every colour got its fair share in a rainbow. I turn my head and am sick again. A hand rubs my shoulder.

The sky is darker by the time I realise it's Sam sitting with me, his dark face full of understanding, I want to slap him. I attempt to roll onto my feet to get away and he helps me up, I shrug him off almost drunkenly. I go back inside, leaning against first the door then the wall as I do so.

I see my parents back in the chairs they ran from earlier, holding each other, and I slip down the wall I was leaning on.

A hand holds out a plastic cup of water and I take it, it's from the medical student, he's not looking at me now.

They give us just a few more minutes before they bring someone over to talk to us.

We'll be able to see her soon. But it's not her anymore.

They'll help us with arrangements. We already made arrangements, we're not surprised, but we're still in shock.

Shock is normal. Obviously.

When they bring over paperwork my mum throws it at them.

I stand a bit away from my parents the whole time we sit there, waiting. I can't bring myself to get any closer, I don't want it to be the three of us, that's not how it's meant to be.

When someone comes to take us to another room to see her, she keeps her distance from my mum. I feel the ghost of a dark smile drift for a moment onto my face.

I hover in the doorway most of the time we're in the room. My dad holds her hand while my mum presses kisses to her forehead, cheeks and nose. I only enter the room fully as they go to leave.

I can't touch her. I take the seat that they've laid out near her head and try to breathe.

"I've made a decision." I start, my voice shaky. "There's going to be a bench. In a park, or on a hill or something, and this bench is going to have one rule. If you sit on it, you have to tell a story. To the person you're with, to a stranger, to the birds or the air, you have to tell a story. I'll always tell you stories, about what I'm up to and how I'm doing, and I'll tell you about the pixies and the sirens and the princesses and the monsters. But we're also going to have that bench, and make sure that more stories are told because of you."

I move up in my chair and as I stand, I press a final kiss to my little sister's forehead, but I don't say goodbye as I walk out the room and out of the hospital completely.

CHAPTER 36

I'm at their house before I know it. I ran here, I didn't try and find Sam, I didn't want him to help me but I'm still here. I don't know why.

It's Lily that opens the door, her face so much paler than normal that I know she knows, I look away from her empathetic, understanding eyes. I look past her into the entrance, it looks grey.

Stepping past her now, I see that the light in the hall has dimmed, I still can't see any source for the light but it seems to have lost half its oomph. I know how it feels. Maybe it's how they feel.

Knowing that Lily knows, I feel like they all must. I look around, half expecting Ivy to barrel into me in an all-encompassing hug of comfort, she doesn't.

"Where is everyone?" I ask, expecting my voice to crack like it has been doing since, since it happened, since before it happened, when it was on the horizon.

Lily's eyes flash for the first time since I've known her and for the instant they do, the light in the hall blinks lower and a tinge of red passes like a film over my sight.

"They're not here." She answers, voice harder than I thought possible, bitterness laced through.

I blink at her. "Where are they?" If not here, where? They are always here, whenever I have come to this house, most of them have been here, they are always here.

Lily shakes her head, pale blonde hair bouncing, the light in the room bouncing. "I mean, they are here, they're in the building but you can't see them Will." I just stare at her, confused at this rule she's laying down. At the look on my face, she shakes her head faster and the lights blink more rapidly. "No, Will, I mean you shouldn't see them they're not taking it well."

She stops shaking her head when she stops speaking and looks at me apologetically. The lights return to their stable grey hue.

I let out a short, hollow laugh, which bounces around the large room. I listen for where it bounces against each wall before I return my attention to Lily. "They're not taking it well?" My voice is not as incredulous as I expect, I can't muster enough of it.

Another short laugh escapes me, then a small scream, it erupts up from my stomach, rumbles through my windpipe, climbs out my mouth and explodes. I listen to it echo like the laugh. I find it satisfying and do it again, I'm still so full of screaming.

"Will?" The voice is so small, it comes to me from far away and I turn towards it, away from Lily.

Ella stands halfway up the staircase, eyes so full of every kind of sad. My head arcs back and another short scream escapes.

When I lower my head back down and open my eyes, I'm no longer in the entrance room. I'm on a cliff.

Wind whips at my face and makes me gasp for breath. The cliff is long and narrow, I stand right by the edge, overlooking crashing waves, far, but not far enough, beneath me, I can almost feel the spray of the water. Lily stands beside me but she moves away, like a ghost fading to translucence, as Ella reaches me. She holds my face in her hands and tries to capture my gaze in hers. I try to fight it.

I fall to my knees, still trying to catch my breath from the whipping wind, Ella falls with me, slipping onto her own knees.

"Will." Her voice is stronger than I've ever heard it, slicing through the wind, right through me. "Will, I need to listen to me. I need you do to do what I say. I'm here and I know what you're going through."

I rage against her, like the waves below me. She may have lived forever, they all may have, they could have lost every kind of love but they didn't know this pain. How could they, they kept going. You can't keep going after pain like this, I can't keep going.

"Will. Breathe." Ella's voice demands.

I can't. "I can't."

"Breathe."

I do, just.

"Now, take a breath and breathe in all this pain."

I stop breathing again. "No, no, no."

"Take in all you can in one breath, Will. Do it."

I breathe in, and I try. It all crashes into me, the resounding noise that I never thought my mother capable, the doctor's stopping their movements, their efforts, the eyes of that medical student, so full of 'I'm sorry'. I gasp the breath out, I can't do this.

Ella's hands clamp tighter onto the sides of my face. "No, Will. Breathe it in and hold it. Please." Her voice finally breaks at the end, it cracks open and I see how scared for me she is.

I breathe again. I see Katie laughing, hear her laughing, feel her cuddled against me, smell the hospital, taste the sick in my throat. I want to choke it all out but I try and hold it. I feel like I'm suffocating.

The next word Ella speaks is all I need to hear.

"Scream."

I do.

I scream and scream and scream. The wind rushes away from me, propelled by my voice. The water rushes in waves away from the cliffside, away from me.

I pause and breathe in again. More thoughts bombard me, my dad reading aloud to Katie, my mum making pancakes with her, Ian twirling her over his head. I scream again.

Eventually I run dry, I run out of screaming, but I still feel drowned, too full.

Ella still holds my face, her hands, she, never left me.

"Now I want you to breathe in all the anger."

My eyes find hers. She holds them steadily.

"It's ok if it's at us."

I breathe again, and it is them, all of them that flash across my mind, everything they did for Katie that wasn't enough. The anger that they could give her more laughter, my parents more peace, but none of us more time. I hold it and feel like I'm bubbling over.

Ella's hands caress over my cheeks before she says her next words.

"Now, cry."

I do.

Right into her shoulder, I cry, and wail and empty. After I let out all my thoughts of them, I'm left with just me and Katie sitting on her bed, her most of the way to sleep as I tell her a story, and then the final anger hits me, that I couldn't give her more time either, that I couldn't swap places. I cry until I'm run dry again, completely.

And then I sleep.

CHAPTER 37

I wake up with no idea how long I've slept. I don't feel rested. I'm in a bed, bigger than a king, with pillows of every shape and a duvet that is weighing me down in place.

Clumsily I move the duvet off of my torso and sit up. Ella sits in a fabric tub chair, a little away from the bed I lie in. Her legs are crossed over each other and she's tapping her knees with her fingers, arms resting on the high sides of the chair. She smiles as I look at her, I manage to lift the corners of my mouth at her.

"We called your parents." She says, before it can even dawn on me to worry about that, I just vanished on them. I nod and sigh in relief, rubbing my hand over my face.

When I drop my hand back down, Ella has moved to perch on the side of bed nearest me. I look around the rest of the room, there are different sizes of chairs and bookcases shoved into the many nooks and crevices of the room, I see a pin board decorated with the tickets and receipts of days out, most of which I went on with her, and the rest of the walls are decorated with different knick-knacks; odd tiles and wallpaper strips, paintings and clocks, hats and mirrors. There's something warm about the haphazard layout, I keep looking at it as Ella keeps looking at me. I think I'm in her room. I never thought of them having rooms before. I bet Cara's is full of hanging fabrics and antique lamps.

Finally turning my head back to Ella I don't know what to say to her. I don't know what I'm thinking. I feel empty.

"I know." Is all Ella says, and this time I believe her.

"I don't know what to do." I admit, half asking her to tell me what to do.

"You don't have to know that right now." She says, her voice is all gentleness.

After a moment Ella stands and I stand and move with her out of the room. We enter into the normal entrance hall, still with its grey light, onto the landing at the top of the stairs, I turn to look at the doorway leading into the room with all the pictures but Ella takes my hand and guides me away from it, whispering, "Not yet." We go downstairs.

Ella takes me through a door into a kitchen and places me on a stool waiting at the island of the kitchen. It's a beautiful room, if kitchens are your thing, lots of clear counter space and sparkling, hanging utensils and pots, with a nice wood finish to everything. Drawing a chopping board out of a hollow space in the central island, Ella takes fruit of all kinds out of the two-door retro style fridge and begins to chop them up.

"I'm not hungry." I say.

"It's not food." She says.

As she chops I understand why she's doing it, the rhythm is soothing, and some movement is better than none, it's like when we first talked in my flat. I don't make a move to help her though, I just let my eyes slip out of focus as she continues chopping, until I just see blurs of colour and listen to the calming methodically thumping of the knife against the board.

The fruit is scooped into a number of boxes before being placed back into the fridge and Ella moves onto chopping vegetables. It's only when I blink my eyes back into focus that I notice, a large pot is sizzling on the hob behind her.

"What is that?"

"Soup."

I nod, and then slowly stand to move around and peer into

the pot. The smell of homemade soup wraps around me as I near it and I find myself wrapping my arms around Ella as she turns to place the next chopped vegetable into the pot. Her arms curl around mine, and we stay there.

We pull apart when my phone buzzes in my pocket. I pull it out despite not really caring to know the source of the noise. It's a text from Ian, "I'm here." I know he doesn't mean he's at my house, or outside the door or anything, he's heard and he's here for me. I press to call him, Ella continues chopping.

"Hey." Ian says quietly when the call connects.

"Hey."

There's silence, and I close my eyes against it, almost able to see Ian's mouth try and find the words, eventually he settles on the fact there aren't going to be any that are right and just says what he's thinking.

"She was the best kid ever."

"I know."

Silence flows between us again, after living in it for a while, Ian ends the call. I lower my phone back to my pocket.

I need to think about something. "What are the others doing?" In my question I hope Ella can hear the plea for explanation, for enough to be said it finds a place in my head, so it's not still all taken up with this numb pain, the ache pulsing with my heart.

Ella answers my plea. "Danny is in the gym, punching things. Sam and Lily are together, trying to get it together. Cara is in the bar, practicing her cocktail making skills. And I have no idea where Ivy is."

Punching things, drinking, and being lost, they all sound like good options. "How are you here?" I ask, confused by how composed Ella is, suddenly.

She looks at me before answering, like she's not sure of the answer. "You needed me." She says, the words falling from her lips.

I kiss her. We've held hands and her lips have brushed my cheek but I've never kissed her before. I hold her face while I do, and her hands slowly move up to hold my forearms. I don't know how long it is before I pull away but I hold my eyes shut for another moment, giving myself time to fall back to Earth.

As I open my eyes, I see that Ella's eyes are only just opening too and feel the corners of my mouth turn up again, briefly.

"I have to go home." I say, Ella nods.

CHAPTER 38

I stand on the street for a while before I manage to get through the door. My mum and dad are standing in the kitchen looking like ghosts of who they were. I'm still in the doorway when they spot me, my mum tries to smile but it doesn't quite get to her face.

The house is too quiet, too peaceful, it should match how we feel. The lights should all be grey and flashing, like their house was, the floor should be shaking and the walls crumbling, but instead the house stands as it always has.

I had expected my mum to be busying herself like she always does, to have a list and be shouting at me and my dad to work through it, but she's just standing there, they both are.

Properly stepping into the kitchen with them I open the fridge and find what I'm looking for, I pull out a chopping board and start to chop just like Ella had.

"I thought I'd make soup." I say, voice so flat it falls right to the floor.

"You don't know how to make soup." My mum returns, voice falling too. She steps forward as well and takes a pot out of a cupboard, and a measuring cup for water.

My dad reaches for a cook book above the hob and starts rifling through it for a recipe that matches the ingredients we have.

We cook in silence, apart from my dad's occasional adjusting us to follow the recipe, when the background stuff is done, my mum joins me in the slow chopping of vegetables and I see tears running down her face. I pull out an onion next and start chopping that, giving her an excuse, though we hardly need one. I cut through the skin of it and as the smell mixes with the rest wafting through the kitchen, it's like an allowance. My parents start to cry, and I let them, I move around them and feel my eyes sting as well, sure more tears will come later.

We don't eat the soup, once it's finished we place it in plastic boxes and distribute them between the fridge and the freezer.

Ian arrives, and knocks on the door instead of ringing the bell, I think he's trying not to disturb our silence. I let him in and he shuffles into the living room, resting himself on the sofa and staring into space. He must've hated feeling like this alone. I sit with him and we don't talk. My dad comes in and turns on the tv, it's on some channel showing reruns of old sitcoms, we all stare at the screen without watching and my mum joins, sitting on the arm of my dad's chair and holding his shoulder, to keep them both upright. It makes me think of Lily and Sam, being together, to get it together.

That's how we pass most of our time, between then and the funeral.

CHAPTER 39

All the arrangements have been made. We only make one slight adjustment. Changing Katie's outfit to the dress the girls gave her during our picnic in the gardens.

The whole thing takes place outside, chairs are arranged by the hole that lies there ready. My stomach turns over when I catch sight of it, and I can't keep it out of my periphery. My mum and dad are standing at the back of the area we're set up in and are shaking people's hands as they arrive, they asked if I wanted to join them, but I took my seat instead.

When Ian arrives, he perches on the seat next to me for a while and I try telling him to just take the seat properly. I think he's sitting like that because he doesn't feel like he should sit in the front row, with the family, but he is family.

I'm wrong though, about why he's on edge like he is, he's waiting, now he stands and I swivel partially in my seat to see which arrival has driven him to get up. It's the others, they're in a clump of people shaking hands with my parents, and as I watch I see Lily gives my mum a tight hug. Ella moves away from the group, over to me and Ian, she's wearing a simple black dress, free of all embellishment except for a blue ribbon tied around her waist.

Katie had given strict instructions that everyone had to be in colour on the day, she liked colour and would not have it be denied for any reason. I wore a tie she'd picked out herself, it was somewhere between pink and magenta in colour. She had picked it up and declared it fuchsia before shoving it in my hand, she'd loudly pronounced it "Few-sha!"

I remember that clearly as Ella walks over to us, she smiles at Ian and he moves to let her into the space between us, he'd apparently been saving the seat for her. Ella takes my hand as she says hello and softly kisses my cheek. "I'm here. All day, okay?"

I nod at her, tears brimming in my eyes, but I don't let them fall. Today, if I start crying, that'll be it, I squeeze her hand instead.

The rest of their group come up along the row of seats behind us, Ian moves around next to them. Cara, Ivy and Lily are all wearing black dresses in their own style, each with colour threaded through somehow, Cara with red jewelled jewellery and a red hairband, Ivy with multi coloured hair, and Lily with pale gold detailing on the pattern of her dress. Sam wears a suit with a shiny green tie, and I see no colour on Danny until he adjusts his sleeve and I catch sight of the sweet bracelet still on his wrist.

We don't say anything as we take our seats but I feel them there. I also spot, just in my line of sight, Cara slipping out a hip flask and taking a swig, before offering it to Ian.

I don't know how long it takes for everyone else to arrive, distant family and family friends come over to whisper good sentiments to me and I nod at them, focussing on Ella's hand in mine all the time. Felix comes over and holds my shoulder for a moment before moving over to find his seat, as his eyes slide over the hole in front of us I can see regret for moving away in his eyes. He was my best friend and almost another brother of Katie's, like Ian, I can't bear the look in his face. I move my free hand up to hold his arm before I let him go and he gives me a brief, sad smile.

I see Isaac and his boyfriend slip into the back, the seats have filled up so they just stand, I see faces from my lunch table at university standing with them, none of them ever met Katie. I appreciate them coming anyway.

The service starts, I know everyone expects me to talk, I can almost feel it, palpable, in the air, but I told my parents I didn't want to. Everything I needed to say, I had said, and it wasn't for everyone to hear. I didn't know what I would've said to anyone else.

To mine, and my parents surprise, towards the end of the officiator speaking he invites Ian up. We twist around to see him move up front, and he looks at us as he does, silently checking if it is ok. My mum reaches out her hand to him when he reaches her and she tugs him down to her level for a moment, I hear her whisper in his ear. "You were her favourite uncle after all."

Ian's eyes are glistening as he reaches the front. "I'm not much for speaking." A quiet rumble of laughter erupts from our friends and I'm surprised to hear my dad join in. "Well, not about important things." Ian continues. "And today is certainly that, but the feelings we all have for today are difficult to express. So I've got a pretty unorthodox idea for what we could all do, for Katie."

Before Ian continues, I hear the group behind me start to move, but don't look around, I can't take my eyes off of Ian. I feel Ella slip something into my free hand and see my parents both handed something as well, glancing down I see a pink balloon resting in my hand, waiting to be blown up.

"I thought we could all blow up our balloons, thinking about Katie, and then we'd have a kind of representation of the colour she brought to our lives." Ian's voice tales off as he finishes speaking and I see him worry that this is a stupid idea, that we'll all stare at him blankly, but I can't think of anything more perfect.

I raise the balloon to my lips and start to blow it up, Ella and my mum on either side of me do the same and then the air is filled with the sound of all our breath. And then the space is filled with so much colour.

Me and Ian share a long hug when the service ends, and I feel my parents join it behind me. We don't watch the casket be lowered into the ground, we all agreed a long time ago, it wasn't something we could bear to watch, and I know it was the right decision, seeing the hole is enough.

We all start heading back to my house, and I retake Ella's hand as we go.

CHAPTER 40

It's three weeks before I ask Ella if we can go and see the picture of Katie that they have put in the room upstairs. We're playing a game of pool and I feel the urge to see it, and it's because I want to see what kind of picture they used more than anything else, which is why I finally ask, finally feel ready to ask.

Ella's eyes scan my face before she agrees. We stop right in the middle of our game to go and see. We play pool so much we've stopped keeping track of who is winning between us overall, though we still dorkily celebrate every win over the other.

Danny and Cara are passing through the entrance when we enter it and Danny immediately eyes us so speculatively that I think he must know where we are heading, but when he eyes Ella's and my, clasped hands, I realise he's just being protective of her, still. He doesn't need to worry, I vividly remember his threat not to hurt her.

"We're heading upstairs." Says Ella, after we pass hellos around each other, the one between Danny and I, just a grunt.

Cara's eyes scan over my face in the same manner as Ella's. "We'll come too." She says, leaving no room for Danny to back out, so he doesn't.

We move up the stairs together, Cara telling me about the A she had gotten in English. I had indeed missed out on doing my exams, and am resitting them in a couple of months. Apparently with Cara's awesome grade she has decided that nearer the time, she will tutor me, I try to mask my apprehension.

My grip tightens on Ella's hand as we pass through the door. Cara nudges my shoulder before I can have a look around, drawing my attention to her. "We can change it if you like." She says, softly. I then follow her moving gaze and spot the picture, clear as day against the wall.

My eyes prick as I take it in. The picture isn't a photograph, it's a painting. A beautiful painting. Katie is on a swing, laughing, all of the colours around her are so vibrant, she is so vibrant, her eyes shine out of the picture and the laugh on her face is so realistic, I can almost hear the sound just looking at it.

"Don't change it." I manage to whisper.

"We won't." Says Danny behind me, and I hear the echo of his promise of 'forever' in his voice.

I stare at the image for a long time, and feel Ella's hand leave mine as she exits the room to give me space. Danny's footsteps retreat as well, and I expect Cara has left the room as well.

However, when I finally turn my back on the painting, ready to leave the room, Cara stands, leaning against the doorways, looking at me, smiling.

"What?" I ask, unable to decipher what lies behind the smile she's giving me.

"I'm just glad I brought you here." She keeps smiling.

I return it now. "Yeah, did I ever say thank you?"

Cara laughs, "Definitely not at the start."

I remember back to how I'd felt that first time in this house, it was a world away from how I feel in it now, I laugh as well, before another thought tugs at me. "Wait, you never explained how I remembered you all, people are meant to forget when they leave the house right?"

Cara's face squishes in confusion for a second before

she continues her laughing. She leans forward, still leaning against the doorframe, and dramatically whispers. "Ella." It's like she's planning on leaving it at that but at my bemused expression she continues. "Ella saw you that first day you were here, she saw something in you. Wanted to give you a chance."

I feel warmth spread through my chest as Cara's words wash over me, so happy with the new knowledge that Ella saw me first, and cared a little bit, first. I also like how pink her cheeks will go when I tell her.

I'm grinning, when a cloud passes in front of the light in Cara's eyes and my eyebrows crinkle. "What?"

"You remember the rules I gave you?" She says, voice timid now.

That is another easy one to remember, Cara making our whole lecture theatre filled with people, freeze as she laid down the law. Though I can't remember the exact rules, apart from not telling anyone else. That has become a little trickier to want to keep, as Ian gets to know everyone as well, but I haven't said anything.

I'm racking my brain for the other rules when Cara sighs and helps me out. "You can't remember forever Will. It never works when people know about us properly. You can't live in the real world and in ours."

I blink at her. "No, but it's fine."

"It's the rules, you agreed."

"That was before, everything, I didn't think I'd have so much to remember. I didn't think you'd all become what you are." My voice is stretching my meaning out to her, cracking at the effort.

Cara's eyes stay clouded over, in sadness I see now, sadness and resolution.

"When?" I ask, a plea for her to say some time way down the line, years from now, decades.

The cloud in her eyes starts to rain, and a single tear slips down her cheek. "We agreed it would be when you came here." She nods around the room regretfully. "When you were okay enough to come here, then we'd be able to have this conversation.

I'm ready to argue and yell at her, it's just the tear slipping down her face that calms my voice. "You're making me forget you, right now?!"

"Forgot *about* us. Not forget us."

"What's the difference?"

"You'll remember us, that we're friends, that you and Ella are more, that Danny pisses you off, you'll remember all the time you've spent with us, but the memories will shift a bit. Shift into aligning with the real world. We'll became real to you, the way we are for Ian." The way Cara explains it, so clear and concise, it's obviously rehearsed.

I don't want to forget anything, but I can't think of any arguments. I'll still have them. Cara will tutor me, terribly, in English, Danny will still be overprotective, Ivy will still pounce on me in a hug whenever I see her, and Ella, Ella will still be with me.

"You'll have to hide who you are from me." I say, remembering as well that Ivy will not be able to change her face for me, Cara can't do a fashion show of styles without moving, they can't be themselves.

"We hide from everyone, Will. But I promise you, this is the only way we won't lose you." I can hear in her voice that she's ignoring the inevitable loss that comes with time, and talking about not prematurely losing me. There is also a tone of desperation in her tone that I would never associate with Cara, and I can see how much she doesn't want to have this conversation.

Which is the only reason, I'm able to accept that we're really having it.

Ella reappears behind Cara as I finally accept what's about to happen, and she smiles sadly at me, holding her hand out for me to take it. I have to step forward to reach her and Cara takes that time to slip away. Ella guides me out onto the landing and moves me so I stand in front of her door.

I turn my head to see if the others are around, they aren't. "I kind of want to say goodbye."

"This isn't a goodbye." Says Ella, keeping any sadness out of her voice. "It just is."

While we look at each other, I try and remember everything one last time, their pasts that they've shown me, the house they live in, the only place they are always free to be, and appearing/disappearing books, sofas and pianos that I feel some part of me will always miss.

Ella leans up on her toes to kiss me.

And I forget.

EPILOGUE

I kiss Ella goodbye outside her door, and then head out of the house. Going down the little flight of stairs, I speculate for what feels like the hundredth time about how six people manage to live in a little Victorian.

As I'm reaching to open the door, it flings open and I have to spring back to avoid being hit by it, almost knocking over the little phone table they have.

Ivy steps in and makes an oddly shocked look around the room before she sees me. Unsurprisingly, she wraps her arms around me and I catch her laughing. She holds onto me for a long time before letting me go, her face strangely sad. "See ya, Will." She says, her voice upbeat despite her eyes.

I have to run home to see my parents, otherwise I would stay and ask. "See ya, Ivy." I reply, moving passed her out the door. Surely Ella or one of the others will talk to her if she's upset.

I'm stuffing my earphones in my ears as I reach the house's low wall, and almost bump right into someone on the street. I pull one earbud out again, ready to apologise, and take in the sight of a tall, dark haired, blue eyed man, a couple years older than me. He's not even looking at me, just blinking at the house I just vacated.

"Are you here to see Cara?" I ask, she's the only one who ever brings guests to the house, I should know, having been one myself initially.

He looks down at me, forehead too creased for someone so young. "I'm here to see all of them."

I nod, feeling a little uncomfortable due to the intensity of his gaze.

"Well, if you're a friend of theirs I'll probably see you around sometime then. I'm Will." I say as I move passed him and start down the street. Before I turn my music on, I just make out him saying his name to me, before he moves through the gate himself.

"Adam."

Index

Knowing them

7	Chapter 1
16	Chapter 2
22	Chapter 3
27	Chapter 4
35	Chapter 5
39	Chapter 6
47	Chapter 7
53	Chapter 8
58	Chapter 9
66	Chapter 10
71	Chapter 11
78	Chapter 12
86	Chapter 13
89	Chapter 14
93	Chapter 15
100	Chapter 16
109	Chapter 17
115	Chapter 18
121	Chapter 19
124	Chapter 20
133	Chapter 21
137	Chapter 22
141	Chapter 23

144 Chapter 24
150 Chapter 25
157 Chapter 26
161 Chapter 27
166 Chapter 28
175 Chapter 29
179 Chapter 30
183 Chapter 31
191 Chapter 32
197 Chapter 33
202 Chapter 34
206 Chapter 35
208 Chapter 36
212 Chapter 37
216 Chapter 38
218 Chapter 39
222 Chapter 40
227 Epilogue